Dawn Raid

Siobhan Sean Rosenthal

Press

Published by 99% Press,

an imprint of Lasavia Publishing Ltd.

Auckland, New Zealand

www.lasaviapublishing.com

Edited by Rowan Sylva

Designed by Daniela Gast

ISBN: 978-1-991083-10-4

This book is dedicated to my three children, Bradley, Joseph and David, and my sister, Gwendoline.

It is also offered with gratitude to the kaumātua of Mangere Village who so graciously shared their ancestral stories on the Ihumātao front line.

2019

Mangere Village

Yeah, I know you. You're woke, right, aware. You know the score about this Ihumataao bust-up, you've seen us on the news. The flags, the crowds, the awkward-looking police officers. It's Bastion Point all over again, except with mobiles. And bigger crowds.

Poor Bastion Point. Their big problem was, when the end came and the police moved in, they didn't have Facebook. Couldn't call for help. We did.

Who's we, you're asking? I thought this was a white author. Are you getting your Pākehā undies in a twist, now you're realising, white Irish/Jewish name on the outside of this book, brown voices within? Are you hesitating, wondering if it's OK to read, whether this is – shudder - CULTURAL APPROPRIATION?

Don't ask me, I didn't pass NCEA Level One. We called for help and we didn't check the colour of their skin. "We need bodies." That was our live feed, middle of the night, that moment when the police showed up, the demolition trucks rolling in, "we need everyone." ECome down, stand your ground. And yeah it worked, the empty backend of nowhere, between the Sistena plastic factory and the polluted end of the harbour, suddenly it was full. Yoga pants, ecohairies, students, backpackers taking time off from seeing the world... and us. Lots of us. Tangata whenua, and then some. Ihumātao was suddenly Home Turf for every Kiwi with a Māori great-grandmother somewhere in their whakapapa, or at least the ones who were prepared to acknowledge it.

They came in their camper vans, their crappy Warehouse festival tents, their busted up cars. They showed up because they cared, and they were fed up with a century and a half of injustice, and they were here to stay. Which is all very grand and inspiring and all that, but it makes for a shitter of a job cleaning the camp toilets.

You might wonder why I'm talking about the bogs. When there's so many amazing things to say about that time, not least the fact that we fucking eventually won. Well, kind of. We stopped the build, and the land deal is rumbling on, might get sorted finally by the beginning of the next millennium. But you know that. It's a good news ending, isn't it? Sod that though, if I'm gonna write the story of the camp I'm gonna tell the whole truth. The good, and the bad, and the disgusting. And the toilets, frankly, stank worse than the Governor-General's arse. I dunno how we put up with them. I've got no frigging idea how I ended up agreeing to clean them.

That's family pressure for you, right? On my own, I'd have probably focused for the sit-down-and-drink-beer part of the protest action. But I'm not here on my own, and Mum and Nana insist I do my bit. *He rau ringa e oti au*, many hands make light work and all that kinda jazz, they translate it for me because everyone knows unlike the rest of the family I don't know my arse from my elbow in Māori. And that makes me feel like a bit of an outsider, like I've gotta prove myself. Especially here. And when I've only been back six months.

So I sign the bog rota, get up with the early morning light and it's scrubbing gloves on. The smell of the gents makes me wanna retch, so I decide to leave that for the other volunteer and do the disabled wharepaku instead.

Doesn't say disabled, well it does on the Pākehā sign, that's because it's hired from a company that usually makes its big wodge of dough providing places to piss for Kiwi summer music festivals. Dunno if they gave us a discount, but I bet they were thrilled when this kicked off. Who else but a bunch of desperate land pilgrims were gonna go overnighting in an Auckland field in July? Anyway, some clever sod had put up a sign saying Kaumātua, which is cool, right, I mean it's good they got somewhere large and clean to do their business, and it meant all us Māori and most of the rest knew to steer clear, not slip in for a quick piss because the other bogs were long lines. I might have been away from my family for goodness knows how long but at least I know that.

A few German backpackers tried to nip in but our first aid nurse saw, put them straight. So our *Wharepaku o Kaumātua* was clean and good and quiet, just the way it should be. No problem to clean at all. But there was a kinda problem even so, because some of our kaumātua are pretty traditional in their ways, and this Portaloo, it was right up at the end of the line, set away, and almost right by the community meeting place. Which, now we'd not had it consecrated formally as a marae, but that was where it all happened, the singing and the meetings and the prayers, a separate bit from where we ate and shat, at least it was supposed to be. So anyone who has ever been bawled out by their nana on a marae for not washing their hands properly after going wharepaku knows, mixing tapu and noa is a big no no. No Māori would ever have put it there.

The problem is, the company just came and dumped it there, and we couldn't get them to come back and move it. The committee complained, and a drunk man rang them back and said they hadn't realised they were hiring out toilets to an illegal protest, and if we made them come back and move stuff around they'd just take the whole lot back and we could go piss in the river like the savages we were. That was on the phone, of course. They wouldn't put it in writing. Not stupid enough. Was the same with my social worker. She'd say all sorts of nasty patronising stuff in person or phone but her emails were sweet as honey. Never speak to a Pākehā on the phone.

So our extra large disabled toilet just had to sit there, way too close to the king's flag and the microphones. And I know for a fact that some kaumātua from up north refused pointblank to use it, and there was a bit of aggro between them and the stewards who didn't just want us going in the back field. But I'm tryna be positive so let's just be glad that the Māori Wardens turned up with one of their big campervans and anyone who had a problem with the Kaumātua Portaloo was allowed to go and do their stuff in there.

That was not the only kind of shit that turned up in the wrong place. One guy, he was Irish Aussie, had been over the ditch for so many generations he didn't even know which bit of Ireland his people originally came from. He came and set up camp with the rest of us, all well and good, I mean it's not like we check for a mental health certificate at the door. Said it was, like Cromwell had done to Ireland and he wasn't going to stand for it happening again here. So we're multi-cultural and everyone welcome, yeah? But one day he started showing a woodchopper's axe to visitors and saying he'd slash any police who'd turn up with it.

Big no-no. We're protectors, not protestors. All right for him, he was Pākehā. But for the rest of us, we've got to get away from that idea that we're all like the guys in Once Were Warriors, see? So definitely no violence. That was the rule.

Yeah so my sis has just come and looked over my soldier and wants to know how I said *wharepaku o kaumātua*, when any kohanga reo kid knows it should be, *wharepaku o nga kaumātua*, and how come anyway I am writing this shit in English at all. That's all very well for her but some of us didn't get to go to *kura kaupapa* and learn how to speak te reo. It's not my fault that when I was younger mum and dad split and somehow I ended up in care for ten years. It would have been one, but they wouldn't accept that mum was capable of looking after me. So yeah when I turned sixteen I came home, and six months later all this kicked off and we came down here. Along with every other bored lazy bugger in New Zealand. You can tell the real protectors from the lazy arseholes because it's only the genuine ones who care about making dinner and cleaning the toilets.

It's kinda inspiring, though, when you look around. It's like the whole of South Auckland turned up. Not just our people, Asian and Pasifika and Indian and the rest. Migrant Workers Organisation came out in support. We got Irish and Italian and Jamaican flags on site, and half a bunch of Pasific island nations I never even knew existed. The big churches sent folk too, well, some of them, and there was a cool Muslim group who turned up every Friday handing out free curry and soup.

Some Jewish youth organisations came along too, only they kept quiet when our people started singing about Palestine. Yeah, there was this Pākehā cartoonist guy turned up one day to support us, he'd been fired from all the mainstream press for his anti-Israel cartoons. Well, he claimed they were just anti-Israel, but the Jewish crowd reckoned they were anti-Semitic. He came and chatted for ages by the front line, what he reckons is there is this big Jewish conspiracy and it's where all the money is, so the company that is trying to develop the land is probably run by Jewish shareholders. He says the Jews were behind colonialism and now they're behind a lot else too. Apparently they're trying to control the world through vaccines and all sorts of other shit. He went on and on. Eventually one of the stewards heard what he was talking about and sorta rushed him away. It was really weird but also kinda interesting.

1862

The Governor's Residence, Auckland

The plotters did not want their plans leaked too soon. So they met behind closed doors, in the smoking room in the stately governor's house. The walls were adorned with the finest Māori handiworks the Governor had procured. There were feather kahu, kiwi and sea eagle. Or at least the trader had said it was a genuine sea eagle, and why not believe him, even if his eyes had glinted a trifle and when you walked away you found you had been short-changed. Disappointing, later, to find that you'd paid good Empire coin for a bit of dead European pigeon.

That was the problem, you see. These Māori had got so good at playing the merchant's game, they were taking advantage of the colonisers, instead of the other way around. Furthermore, the craftier among them had realized that there were disadvantages to selling their land. This was not the natural order of the Empire, and it needed to be restored. That was why, as they talked, they glanced occasionally at the war clubs that hung on the wall. One in particular drew everyone's eye. A taiaha, beautifully carved. Its eyes were set with shining kauri amber, rubbed and smoked according to tradition to bring immortality and invincibility to the holder. The diamonds of the north. Probably rubbish, of course, but it made sense to buy up as many of these treasures as they could before war broke out. It would be easier to crush the Māori if they believed the mana of their weapons was trapped in the invader's hands.

I'm telling you like I imagine it, I confess. It's not as if I was there. Tom's the name. Tommy, to my friends. Got fewer these days, of course. Mostly it's the rheumatism that keeps me company. And the Sisters of Good Mercy who stop by and try to persuade me back into regular Mass.

The reason I don't go? That's part of the story. You'll meet me later, as a boy. This is my book, see, at least it's the one I'm telling. Have I the right to tell it? Ah now that's a controversy and a half, you'll have time to make your mind up about that before you get to the end. Like you'll decide whether I'm telling the truth about what I saw, and imagined fairly about what I did not. Lads tell tall stories, don't they? Especially us young Irish. Of course, I'm old and whiskery now, spread out around the middle just like Auckland. But when I came out from Ireland it was still a scrubarsed bit of town, smaller than Galway even. The only grand place was where the Governor lived. And I did visit it, later, so what I say now is not all imagination.

Before the planning commenced in earnest, the men drank. They poured whisky, which came in barrels from the north, into pale crystal glasses that were so delicately wrought it seemed a miracle that they had not smashed into pieces during their long journey over the crashing sea. The strong drink warmed their stomachs and lit fire on their tongues so that when the governor spoke, they could barely restrain their eagerness to applaud.

A map of the rich country to their south lay before them on the table. Few of them had traveled there, but already they were drawing lots to divide up the land. The rich volcanic soil of the mountains, the fertile Whanganui banks. And the great Waikato river that lay a snaky ink on the map. Forests rippled in all directions around it. This land would be shaped by European hands. Money would be made. Why, it made the tongue slaver to think of all the timber and mineral wealth that they would find.

The governor outlined the task ahead. The road was

nearly built. A pretext would have to be found to declare war, but that was not going to be a problem. Already great shipfuls of Her Majesty's troops were sailing towards this island at the bottom end of the world. The trap was laid. The Waikato tribes were already uneasy, worried about the road building, and the encroachments and expulsions from the north. They would take the bait soon enough. It was just a waiting game.

"What about the wheat fields?" A question rose from the table.

The Governor wrinkled his brow. "Where in particular? They're growing wheat everywhere now."

"Up by the estuary. Ihumātao, they call it. The first place where the Māori grew wheat, probably the first place they farmed. And precious to them. Fabulous land. If we take that, we strike a blow at their pride."

"Noted," said Grey coolly, "We will deal with the local natives separately. Wait until the Waikato is in flames. Then we will have our moment."

The conversation moved on to what would happen after the war. All were agreed, that this was not the time to wipe out the Māori completely. But there would be epidemics of measles and syphilis, once the soldiers had passed. But even a weakened decimated people would survive in patches. Somewhere would have to be found for the defeated to live. There were the mountains. They were not too profitable. It was poor, scrubby land. Perhaps the dispirited survivors could be driven back to that.

And the children, thought the Governor. Those beautiful native children. Untouched, innocent. Fruit on the tree. When they took Waikato for the Empire, they would have all their children too. To educate, or murder, or –

And they didn't just want the native boys and girls, either. The same fate awaited poor white kids like me. You know, the kind with no one to stand up for us. The young Irish who were transported to Australia for stealing sixpence and took to slaughtering natives there with all the fury that burned inside of them for what had been done to them on the prisons and the ships and – oh, but I'm rabbiting on. You're not going to read any further if you're an innocent child, are you. It's not suitable material for the very young. It was worse what happened to Matua, of course. I'll tell you about him soon.

Outside, the rivers groaned, and waited for the end to begin.

2019

Auckland

The café radio crackled. "Ihumātao protest enters its eighth day, the standoff between protesters and police…"

"Ooh, turn that off," complained one of the elderly customers, pushing her glasses up her disdainful nose. The waitress obediently twiddled the dial. An advertisement for Gardening Care blared out, offering more time enjoying and less tilling your back yard. "That's better. I can't bear hearing about it."

"Couldn't agree more," her paunchy husband agreed, wiping his balding pate with a napkin. "They'll never be satisfied. You give in on one demand, they immediately ask for more. Can't see why police are putting up with it. Send in the army. They sorted it at Bastion Point."

"Hear hear." His wife put down her coffee cup with a military clang. "It's all waiata and apologies these days. And those ridiculous unpronounceable placenames on the news." She looked around the café for agreement.

Adele thanked all the gods in which she did not believe that her mum was out in the main shopping area. Otherwise there would have been an almighty public row. Ben, fortunately, was not the political type. The radio might as well have been discussing pig farming techniques. That's why he was a relaxing guy to hang out with.

At least, until now.

"Can I ask you a question?"

"Sure." Adele shrugged.

"Does te Reo even have a word for -" Ben hesitated, delicately. "I mean, I know lots of words are borrowed from English now. But did they before, I mean, traditionally?"

Adele laughed. But not her usual friendly laugh. It was angry, almost scornful. "Did they what? Shit? Wank?"

Ben blinked. He wasn't shocked by the language. Adele swore more than any other home-schooled teenager he knew. Her aging hippie mother encouraged it. She said swearing encouraged self-expression and independence of mind. That's why she wouldn't send Adele to school, in case she grew to think like every other conformist clone in this ghastly consumerist society.

Ben's mother, by contrast, believed that the world was made in six days, that profanity was of the Devil and that if she prevented Ben going to school he would never come across either swearing or the theory of evolution. Thank goodness for Adele, who had introduced him to both.

No, it wasn't the swearing. It was that Adele was angry, and he didn't know what he'd said wrong. If you didn't know something about another culture, shouldn't you ask?

"Are you asking me because I'm Māori?"

"Well, yes." Ben was baffled. What was wrong with that?

"Look," Adele drummed her fingers on the café table so that the coffee cups rattled. "I know I'm brown. But you've got to understand. I've never met my father's family. I haven't seen him since I was five. The only words of Māori I know are the same as you do, whānau and haka. I'm an Oreo, right? White on the inside." She flicked her hair out of her eyes with a dramatic gesture. Partly to show her impatience, partly because it was getting in her way. Hairdressers were a tool of sexist oppression and the beauty hegemony, at least according to her mother, so they never used them.

"So don't come asking me to play the cultural expert, OK? Go watch Māori TV or something. Put on your tiedye pants and go and join the kids at Ihumātao." She gestured at the radio. "I'm not going to be able to help."

Ben shrugged, embarrassedly. "Sorry. I didn't know." He couldn't tell whether Adele was angry with him for asking, or angry with herself that she didn't know the answers. Probably a mixture of both. She never usually minded his questions. In fact, she was the reason he knew that wanking was both natural and normal, and wouldn't do him any harm. That wasn't what he was taught at home, and - not going to school – there were limited opportunities to find out what anyone else thought. Even the home internet still had child filters on. He wondered if that would ever change. Probably not until he got married and left home. He hoped he'd know enough by that age not to look an idiot in front of his wife.

Adele was different recently. More touchy. It had all started when her father turned up. He'd not been interested in her for years. But apparently Inland Revenue had tracked him down and insisted he started paying child support. That was when the trouble started. He wanted joint custody, and for Adele to be sent back to school. Adele's mum was saying no to both. But there seemed to be a constant stream of lawyers and child psychologists and social workers visiting Adele to check that she was all right, and not being abused. Which was all a bit strange, because according to Adele's mum it was her dad who was the abusive one. He'd beaten her up one evening and that was why she'd walked out. Now he was claiming it had never happened, or if it had it was fine because she was mad. Or something. It was all incredibly tedious and Ben was bored of hearing about it. And frankly, Adele was a lot less fun these days. Always on edge. As if she was half-expecting some police officer to turn up and drag her away.

But that was ridiculous. It could never happen in New Zealand. Not over a row over home school.

Adele gave a loud, theatrical sigh. A signal that she was finished with her strop and wanted to be friends again.

"I'm bored already. And we haven't even started yet. My eyes want to roll up into my head and stay there until this fucking project is done."

"Me too. I hate it when home school actually means work." Actually, Ben rather liked studying. But he knew it was the kind of thing teenagers were supposed to say.

They sat glumly in the Mitre 10 cafe, looking at the incomplete assignment cover sheet. The bright orange decor of the hardware chain store rose around them like a garish oversized soft toy. Their mothers had left them to study together whilst they scoured the aisles for gardening gloves and cut price craft supplies. This is the problem with being home educated, Adele thought. You study much less than in school, but most of it ends up being done while mum shops. At least now she and Ben were both fifteen they each got a cappuccino and a slice. Any younger and they'd be fobbed off with the jugs of free water and half a cookie later if they were good.

"We should never have let them talk us into this. What's the point of being home educated if you have to do assignments? Our only perks are daytime tv, getting up when we want and not doing much."

"Speak for yourself," Ben grunted. "I don't get to decide much. My mum gets me up at seven every morning so we can do Bible study as a family before dad goes to work. And she's just started me on Latin. Latin! I'd rather spend the extra time on calculus."

"You sound as if calculus is more fun than wanking." She spoke more loudly than she intended. The elderly couple who had complained about Ihumātao and were now deeply engrossed in the ornamental flower sale paused in their admiration of the marigold section to give her an admonishing glare.

Ben grinned. "It's not that good. Anyway, I'm not supposed to masturbate, it's a sinful waste, something about the spilling of Onan's seed in Genesis. Mum's quite hot on telling me that, although dad just goes pink and shuts up when she starts going on."

"Well, but do you?"

Ben blushed. "What do you think? I said it was good, didn't I? Just don't tell mum or dad."

"Your secret is safe with me. My mum is so keen on reassuring me that it's healthy and normal she would give me tips on technique if I let her." Adele lowered her voice. "She offered to buy me a you-know-what for Christmas."

Ben shuddered. "Do you know, I think that would be worse."

The eavesdropping marigold admirers gave a loud exclamation of disgust and went over to the café counter. Over Ben's shoulder, Adele could see them gesticulating and pointing at the "No Truancy" signage, the ones from the *Keep Kids Safe In School* campaign all the home education groups were so exercised about. The government and courts were cracking down on truancy, which was fine, but home educators were getting caught up in the sweep, which was not fine. That was apparently why Adele's dad was getting traction with his campaign to get her back into school. He insisted that Adele had no friends and never left the house.

"Have you got your Home Education ID card? I think we're about to get a bit of harassment. Teens being legally educated in public alert."

Ben winced. "No. But I've got my calculus homework." He unzipped his bag. "Scientific calculator here, first year university course material here."

"You won't need to go to uni at all at this rate," Adele pointed out.

"Yeah, well there are advantages to being made to get up at 7 am and work at home."

He waved his maths helpfully at the café assistant. She raised a cheery thumb in response and turned to the elderly marigold complainers.

"It's OK, I know them, they're not truants. Home

educated. Well, yes, but I didn't hear them saying anything inappropriate. You should hear the way some schoolkids in here go on. I see, well if you're really concerned I suppose you could always discuss it with their parents..."

Ben looked alarmed. "I really hope they don't."

Adele laughed. "They can tell Cynthia. She'd be delighted. Evidence for the next court psychologist or social worker that I'm a normal healthy teenager and that not getting to hear dirty stories in the playground hasn't stopped me having a filthy mind."

She glanced across Mitre 10 to where Cynthia – who insisted on being called by her first name, because mother and father were terms that represented the oppression of the patriarchy - stood in a hippie jangle of tiedye skirts and handmade Indian beads.

School didn't happen in Adele's life for long because Cynthia had spent one term failing to get her to school before eleven a.m. When the Principal politely suggested that this was not an optimal time to begin morning classroom learning, she wrote out a home education application form, which consisted entirely of the suggestion that timetables were anti-educational and her daughter would learn better by following the rhythms of the seasons and the stars. Her idea of moral guidance for the teen years was to give a lecture about the ideals and practice of free love, shove a packet of condoms into Adele's bedside drawer and tell her to come and talk to her if she needed help with anything difficult, like how to turn down an unwanted threesome or arrange a quick abortion.

Ben's family spent their spare time writing to Parliament about the sinfulness of abortions and public schooling being permitted in New Zealand at all. There had never been any question of sending Ben or his seven older siblings to school. This was because New Zealand schools are secular and don't teach the Bible, which was really all a decent childhood needed to include. Ben's mum, who only let Adele call her Rosemary once she was in her teens (before that it was Mrs Murphy, thank you very much, you can have an extra cookie if you remember) wrote a home education application that promised to follow a stringent overseas curriculum. The curriculum in question explained how the earth had been created in seven days. It also taught that sisters should obey their brothers in preparation for their future role as godly wives. This was odd, because in practice Mrs Murphy made all the family decisions.

Really, it was very unfair, thought Adele, that she was the one who was constantly being investigated by the authorities and accused of being cut off from the 'real world.' But of course, Ben's parents believed divorce was immoral. They were white and middle class. Oranga Tamariki and the Family Court would never get involved.

"All right, let's get the evil hour over with. We need to choose A Topic. I was thinking something Rosemary would approve of. Like is Satanism a healthy alternative lifestyle."

"Or is single motherhood essentially immoral," Ben shot back. "Cynthia will love marking an essay from you on that."

"Yeah, maybe not. I don't want to get locked out of the house."

Really, given how different their families were, it was astonishing that Ben and Adele were encouraged to be friends at all.

The reason, of course, was that dreaded word: Socialisation. Socialisation is what everyone thinks you lack because you don't sit in a hot classroom with thirty other kids you hate. Socialisation is what makes home educating parents pretend they love Scouts and Sea Scouts and Dance and Extra Dance and oh, the Homeschool group. Where all the unschooled kids run around beating up the other ones, and their parents explain they are just free spirits, not feral little sods. As long as you don't mind a few bloody noses, socialisation at that primary age is easy. By the time you are fourteen, though, peer socialisation with other homeschoolers is a lot trickier. Many parents, deliriously in love with their naughty four year olds, are happy to give primary school a miss to enjoy a few more precious years of pillow fights and walks in the park. There are far fewer who are prepared to continue the arduous task of hanging out 24/7 with their monosyllabic and Xbox-addicted teens. Rosemary had got around this problem for years by making her older children babysit and educate the younger ones, but Ben was the youngest and the only one still at home. So Cynthia and Rosemary had developed a friendship of convenience. Ben and Adele hung out together a lot, because both being fourteen they were now the oldest home educated kids in the area.

That meant all the younger ones thought they were dating, which wasn't going to happen for two reasons. Firstly, Ben's family didn't think dating before marriage was Christian. Secondly, although Ben was great eye candy, Adele didn't really want to date anyone yet, she preferred men in movies and books to real life. The problem was, what had happened when she was young was so awful – they'd had to hide out in a Woman's Refuge, and then live at a secret address for ages until he got bored of chasing them around Auckland, and went down to Christchurch to be a couch potato on the benefit there – that she just wasn't sure she wanted to have a man in her life ever, at all. Cynthia had helpfully suggested that perhaps she was gay, but she wasn't sure about that yet.

So Ben and Adele were just friends. At least until their mums got chatting about what they thought the pair needed to broaden their education. It wasn't that they weren't learning. Far from it. Ben hated writing, and had refused to do any on principle since he was ten. It was the only battle he'd ever won at home, and he'd done it by simply swallowing every literacy worksheet he was given until his parents were forced to give up through concern for his increasingly blocked bowels. He was however so good at maths that he had private lessons from a university lecturer, who was also answering his questions about evolution and biology, which had rapidly progressed beyond Adele's *We're all from monkeys and amoebas, dontcha even know that* café explanation.

Adele was great at English literature and French and writing poetry and photography. She could do maths, although she tended not to. She was also secretly quite interested in the philosophy of religion. This she knew better than to tell Cynthia, who believed stridently that religion was the root of all evil except for the patriarchy. Patriarchy was probably worse, although when she discussed this drunkenly of a Friday night it was never quite clear why. Something about the universe having been created by an Arrogant Male Chauvinist who didn't even have the courtesy to make sure men had to deal with childbirth and periods. Or perhaps that was why there couldn't be a God. Adele wasn't quite sure.

But no matter how good Ben and Adele were at the stuff they enjoyed, they were in need of a bit of Group Learning and Social Studies. Apparently it's teamwork and important socialisation to get out of your pyjamas and sit in a garden centre cafe with another teen to bitch about your assignment.

"Let's do some history. I don't know any New Zealand history."

Ben nodded seriously. "OK. Let's do that. Easy. Not much ever happened here. Treaty of Waitangi?"

Adele groaned. "OK I do know about that. No. Boring. Did that when I was six. What else is there?"

Ben thought. "I don't know, to be honest. I mean, I know about the Elizabethans, and the Egyptians..."

"Did we even have any wars here?"

"I think so. Small ones. Not many people died."

A vague memory of a picture book she'd had years ago swam into Adele's mind. It belonged to the stage when

Cynthia still thought her Māori culture could be sort of transmitted by osmosis. There had been a te Reo picture dictionary on the lounge table, and Māori TV on in the background. Adele had ignored them both After a while, Cynthia had given up, and the picture dictionary had gone to a yard sale.

"Kupe. That explorer. The first one who came to New Zealand. Before Cook. We could do something about him."

Ben shook his head. "Kupe's not real. He's a legend."

"You sure about that?" Adele joshed. "You believe in Noah, right?"

"Well. My mum and dad do. I'm still making up my mind."

Ben chewed his lip. It made him look older. And unexpectedly, quite good looking. Perhaps she wasn't gay. Or perhaps she was bi. Perhaps it just wasn't time. Perhaps, at the right moment, if Ben - Adele brushed aside the irritating thought and focused sternly on the history project as a distraction. "Where are your family from?"

"South Waikato. And Hamilton."

"Well, mine are from North Waikato and Awhitu."

"Not your mum. She's Irish. Like my family. Except the ones who are Scottish, of course."

"Yeah I think she's still in rebellion from her Catholic childhood. I'm going to get baptised on my eighteenth birthday just to annoy her."

Adele pushed back her hair again, which was getting into her eyes. She hoped it looked like a businesslike necessary hair flick and not a seductive and frivolous one.

"So anyway, I think we should do something on family history."

Ben looked at her with surprise. "You want to do something about being Māori?"

Adele snorted. "No. I wouldn't know where to start." Anger flared up, a sulky grief that hung heavy and irritable in her stomach. "Didn't I just tell you that, to stop going on about it?"

She tried not to think about why this made her so angry. It was so...weird. To be brown and look Māori, and yet not to speak a word of te Reo, or to know even a single member of her Māori family. Whānau was everything, in Māori culture, and she didn't have it. She didn't know who she was. She might as well have been descended from a cardboard box. An imposter, that's what she was. Not a real Māori person. Just a fake. It made her angry, and sad, and guilty, at once. But Ben was looking stricken and embarrassed, and she realised she had gone too far.

"We could do Irish. We've both got bits of that."

"Yes, that's a good idea." Ben whistled. "Actually there's this old box in our basement, it's got diaries and letters and newspaper cuttings. No one's looked at it for years."

It was odd, now he thought about it. He wondered why not. Then he remembered. At the bottom of the box was a carving. Well, not exactly a carving. More an intricately decorated weapon. It was a type of taiaha, with a particularly striking wood with a polished silken sheen and amber-coloured gems set like eyes in the sharpened tip. No one knew where it came from but it had been in the family for generations.

Once his mum had tried to burn it. She'd been very influenced by a sermon from their latest pastor, who thought Māori traditional carvings might reference pagan gods, and as such served the Devil and shouldn't be in a respectable Christian house. His dad pointed out that was all very well but the reality was that if they were caught destroying or selling a traditional taonga they could have thousands of dollars in fines. He suggested a museum. Mum said that the evil spirits of devil worship would be freed to continue their noxious work of influencing innocent museumgoers over her dead body. Eventually they agreed that the taiaha would stay in the attic until they decided what to do. That was seven years ago. It was probably still there.

Adele whooped, like one of those Red Indians in the books passed around by home schooling families that you couldn't find in public libraries these days. The ones that showed them grateful for Christian missionaries teaching them civilised ways.

And that old box, my friend, is the best news *ever*."

"Yeah, interesting, great historical resource for further investigation..."

"No, dumbass. It means we can quote great chunks of old diaries in our assignment and do much less of our own work."

Ben opened his mouth to say something withering about the smartest students being those who did their own work and didn't rely on dead people to do it for them, when a red haired figure dressed in bright orange whirled up to the table. "Look, Mum! My friends!" it shrieked, and gave Adele a big sloppy kiss. She disentangled herself with difficulty. Ben groaned. Trouble, it appeared, had arrived.

2019

Mangere Bridge

I tried to pull the same trick the next morning. But when I turned up yawning with my bucket, and made straight for the disabled toilet, the old biddy who was organising the rota said not to worry with that, I'd done such a good job yesterday and anyway, it was hardly being used.

So I had to do the gents instead. Gross.

I ended up retching on the side of the road, vomming up yesterday evening's communal boil-up into the tractor tracks. A policeman watched me from the other side of the road. They've got their own house up there, well not theirs exactly but the old farmhouse. Scheduled for demolition, but they've moved in for now. Some wag stuck a notice on the fence explaining it's a 1930s villa in the California style, that it's an old building of potential historical interest, and deserves protection too.

I tried to keep the vomming as quiet as I could, because it was karakia time. Leaders and wardens, they meet every morning under the flagpole, raise the Kīngitanga flag and say a bit of a blessing.

Now don't take this as gospel, but word on the ground is that Mister Royal Kīngitanga's played a bit of a double game with the occupation. One minute he's all over us, inviting the leaders to his coronation ceremonies. Next he's saying to the media that we should be listening to the wisdom of the elders at the marae. Go home. Or at least one of his advisers did. But then he flip-flopped again, when it was clear that the country was grumbling and no matter what the local Māori dignitaries said, the people as a whole didn't want Ihumātao to give in. So now we've got his flag and his support.

I'm not going to say, don't karakia. How do I know if it works or not? Mostly I don't believe in Atua and all that. You don't, when you've been in care, and especially not when you've seen how the people who treat you worst are the ones who're bigging up their church attendance and all that to the social workers. But I've nothing against prayer, if you wanna do that, fine by me. But I don't like all this yoyoing the flag business. Like it was a god, or he is. Straight up, there was no Māori king before the British came and I don't see why we've got one now. I see it this way, the Kiingitanga's a boss like all the others. Just because someone's brown like you, doesn't mean they've got the heart to do what's right. That's one of the things I learnt from my time with the ministry. Coconuts, that's what we called the staff. Brown on the outside, but white within.

Then I saw something strange. There was this old taiaha propped up against the fence. Gorgeous old thing it was, sorta shiny. Bit like paua shell, but it was all wood. I dunno how they'd done it. And it was set with amber stones, like my old cat's eyes. But it was kind of bigger than you'd expect it to be. Like it wasn't gonna be wielded by a man, but a couple of them. Or a giant.

It reminded me of one of those stories my Nana told me when I was small. Way back, our family were rangitira. Yeah, I know every single Māori kid will tell you the same, but straight up this was true. We were in charge of Waikato. Or a bit of it, anyway. Maybe Port Waikato. I don't remember the details. Anyway. One kid ran off north to fight the British. To Auckland. Stole a taiaha from his dad's storehouse. Was going to use it to smash the Governor's head. Only when he got there he was hungry, and he had no money, so he sold it to some dealer and came home.

What he didn't know was, that wasn't any ordinary taiaha. It was sacred, came with us from Hawaikī. Was given to our great great great whatever by Kupe himself. Yeah, I know, load of old cobblers if you ask a Pākehā - but that's the story. Since then our family's had bad luck. The thing is, if you get a blessing like rangitira or leadership or even an antique taiaha, you gotta look after it. Otherwise you'll never do well. That's what my nana said, anyhow. I don't know if I believe it, but I do know my life's been shite so far.

So when I saw this taiaha I sort of blinked, and wondered, just for a moment, if maybe it was the one, the one we ought to get back, and if so, what should I do. But as I was thinking about it, this Pākehā stiff in a pinstripe suit comes out of the police house, strides over to the fence, picks it up like he owns it – which maybe he does, at least according to the law – and goes back. Slings it under his arm, just like a briefcase containing all the paperwork for demolition. And I'm left outside in the ditch, staring at my own vom and wishing I'd got less of it on my shoes.

Only just for a moment, there was something else. I mean I haven't been on drugs at all while I've been here – now the Māori wardens are onsite, this place is about as legit as a Sunday School camp. Maybe they turn a blind eye to a bit of weed at the weekends, round the campfire, but definitely nothing more. And besides, I'm at home now, going straight for my mum's sake, it's not like when I was in the youth residence and wanted to beat the hell out of myself with meth and spirits and anything else I could get my hands on. Hadn't even eaten any of the pukurau, that's magic mushrooms to you, they were passing around in the student tents last night.

So it wasn't like I was hallucinating, or at least I don't think I was. But just for a moment, the ground all the way up to the police house wasn't soil any more. It was maggots. Little white squirming things, wriggling up from nowhere. Like the earth had just split open and upchucked itself too.

And then I had a massive splitting headache, and a couple of moments afterwards the maggots were gone.

"What's it mean if you dream of maggots?" I asked my sis, later, when we were squashed up on the hard benches waiting for the beginning of morning meeting. She shrugged, chewing on a mouthful of the fancy bread some Jewish kids had dropped off to the protest kitchen that morning. Tastes good on its own, but even better with Camembert, which a bunch of organic farmer hippies had brought us up too. Say what you want about camping rough in winter, at least we were getting well fed.

"Ask Nana. Probably you had too much of that boil-up last night. You're a fat pig, you know that?"

I opened my mouth to tell her to get knotted, but then the stiff in a pinstripe suit saunters past and my heart does a flipping backwards somersault. Because now he was close, I knew him. Old Thin-lips, we used to call him at the residence. I didn't know if he'd recognise me. He didn't bother to learn our names. Said it didn't make much difference, because we all looked the same.

And the thing was, I was meant to be going straight now. I'd landed in the residence because a social worker said I'd got into too much trouble, was too much work for any decent family to handle. I'd never account for much, she said kindly, not really my fault, I'd been through too much too young, not really realistic to expect me to straighten myself out. Now I was sixteen. I was home. I wanted to prove her wrong. I wanted to be the exception, the kid who came out of care and didn't go straight to jail.

Also, Ihumātao. Peaceful protectors, that was what we were. We took it seriously. Even if they drag you off to the cop shop, don't fight back we reminded each other every morning, before we went up to the front line. But that bastard. Maggoty eyes, maggoty mind. I'd sworn if I ever laid eyes on him once I was out of the youth residence, I'd beat out his bastard brains.

1862

Port Waikato

A stone skimmed across the water. Then another.

"Who threw that?" Matua looked up from the boat.

Thomas shrugged. "Who knows? Probably just some farm lads."

Matua jutted his chin out scornfully, and threw an arm towards the distant shore, where rows of newly planted settler trees jutted sharply. "From the bank? Not possible. That's four hundred yards, at least. Maybe more. No Pākehā can throw that far."

Thomas stepped delicately away from the bait. Matua was bigger than him. The water was cold, and he didn't fancy another dunking. Anyway, they wouldn't get any fishing done if they started on about politics. "Maybe some of you lot then."

"Us lot?"

"You know. Natives."

Matua's face dropped into a scowl. "There are none of us left on that side. We've all been driven out." Matua jabbed the end of his net into the water violently, as if Governor Grey himself might be lurking in the green depths.

"Maybe that's why we're having no luck today. The latest news is they've expelled the local fish for not swearing loyalty to the Crown."

The moment of tension between them passed, as Matua laughed appreciatively. "They'll be banishing the river next."

"Let's drift for a bit. Let the current find us some dinner."

Behind them sprawled Port Waikato, the houses heavy and placid. Leaden skies coloured the wide waters a dull grey. They drifted for a while. But still no bite.

Matua sighed. "I should have known better than to let me talk you into it. It's not the right day of the month to go fishing. I can't take them home anyway, even if we catch them."

"What'll you do with them?"

"If Tangaroa gives me a catch, I'm selling them to the soldiers. As long as no one at home finds out." He splashed the water by his side, which glittered consolingly as if to promise secrecy.

Thomas nodded tactfully, as if it were totally normal to sell food to the opposing side in a war.

Matua scowled, as if he had sensed his thoughts. "I'm not like my brother, if that's what you're thinking." Matua was clearly upset, so the boys were silent whistle and looked downriver again.

When Thomas spoke, he was calmer. "Food's not going to make any difference one way or another. It's not like selling – something, precious, tapu I mean, like that." He knew better than to mention the name of the lost object aloud.

Matua had a strained expression on his face. Either he was stricken by the memory of the sacred amber taiaha or he was suddenly busting for a piss. When he eventually answered, it was in a slightly strangled voice. "When the Jews left Egypt, they had nothing. But the Lord worked in mysterious ways. Swept down on them with a great mighty spirit of protection. That's what Mum says when Dad gets upset about it."

Thomas puzzled out the reference. It took a while, because they didn't do much Old Testament in Sunday School. "Is she a Christian?"

"No. But she wants to convert, I think. She says the

tohunga's spells don't work as well anymore and we should try the foreign medicine instead. But she won't swear allegiance to the Queen. The rumours up north are that the pakeha want Ihumātao."

"Where's that?"

"Special place, first place we landed, old Hape, dragged himself ashore with his crippled leg...." Matua's voice trailed off into wisps of awkward silence that mirrored the drifting boat.

Thomas remembered Matua wasn't supposed to share tribal stories with outsiders. Bit like when Pa got drunk, and Ma as terrified someone would find out how he danced on the dining room table and broke it. On a Sunday, no less. He wondered if the stories he wasn't allowed to hear were too sacred or too rude for foreign ears. Probably a bit of both.

Matua sat up and grinned. "Anyway. We're not at war yet. It may not come to that. And I hope it doesn't. I don't want us to have to kill each other before we've even had a chance to make a stitch with a few wahine. That reminds me, your sister, is that Mr James still courting her?"

"No, thank heavens." Thomas latched onto the new subject with relief. He remembered the lanky bespectacled schoolmaster who had hung hopefully around the farmhouse last winter with flowers and poems. Like a horny tomcat. "He's given up. Going away soon to that new boarding school they're starting for natives down south, he says. They've offered him a good salary and the head of a boarding house. He says the Anglican Church want as many British-born teachers as possible to instil proper colonial discipline." He gave an involuntary shudder at the thought of Mr James and his thin-lipped ideas of discipline.

Matua twisted his hand around his tiki. "Good riddance. Fuck him. Thin-lips, that's what the Māori kids call him. Or Old Maggot. The way he treats us. As if we're uneducatable savages." He spat, loudly. "Don't forget, white-arse. My father has more schooling than yours."

Thomas' father had come out on the boat from Dublin. He struggled with English at times, and could do little more than write his name. Matua's father had gone to primary school and to a whare Wānanga. He often helped Thomas's father with doing his books. So what Matua said was true, but Thomas wished he didn't feel the need to remind him about it so often.

"Let's fish. Look, shadows there." Matua turned away and stared at the water. "Let's go see what it is."

As the junior in the party, it was Thomas's responsibility to manoeuvre the oars whilst Matua gave directions and speared or hooked their prey. Whilst they talked, Thomas had let the oars rest. They had been drifting across the water. Now they were close to the opposite banks, where the clear fresh estuary water became gloopy with mud. Good for fish, but rotten to row. Thomas wished they'd stayed out in the centre of the river, where the water glowed in the sun, like Matua's suddenly burning cheeks.

The older boy pretended to examine the water to hide his reddening face. "And – she's not seeing anyone else?"

"No."

"Your father, what would he think if I – came over to play draughts with you both one evening? Don't worry, I'd go easy on you." It was worth saying Māori were good at draughts and Matua was better than most, even when they played with the newfangled European rules.

Before Thomas could answer, a group of black mudfish suddenly lurched upwards, towards the surface of the water.

"Hauhau!" screamed Matua. He grabbed a crayfish poraka and wielded it like an axe, chopping through the water. The openmouthed net acted as a sieve. He laughed with delight, holding it up to the sky. "He, this is treasure, better than whitebait." He passed the catch to Thomas. "Well done. First catch with this net."

Thomas groaned. "Does that mean we have to return the whole lot?"

Matua shook his head. "No. Just take one out and do the blood ritual for the river spirits. We can do that on land."

Thomas didn't know what the blood ritual was. He supposed he would soon find out. If it wasn't one of the secret ones, of course. Matua would sometimes insist he shut his eyes and not look. That could mean he was performing some very sacred traditional ritual, or it could mean he was in need of an urgent shit.

Then they were ashore, joyfully, pulling in the boat. The opposite side from the Port Waikato village where they both lived, and a very long journey home when they had rowed up to the great bridge inland where the soldiers had pitched camp to build Governor Grey's Road. A small catch, too, but it didn't matter. Thomas' mother was trying not to buy food as she was saving for new shoes but his were not too tight yet. They would catch an eel sooner or later and that would be food for a week.

Matua didn't bother with shoes, and for him fishing was pocket money, not survival. Matua's family were richer than Thomas's. His father was a resopected leader of the local hapu, and the hapu were good farmers. So good in fact, that they had more stored in the whare taonga than they needed and often gave short-term food charity to those settlers who arrived in Port Waikato with little to their name but seasickness and hope.

So they slapped the sides of the boat with joy for their meagre mudfish catch, and as the Irish folk might have put it, knew that they were blessed. Neither resented the spirits or the river for not providing more. Their spirits were high, and they sang snatches of silly songs as they made for land.

Yes, that was me. Thomas, the happy boy. I'd been in New Zealand only a few years, long enough to think it was paradise, though. Green space, blue skies and good friends. Now I'm an old man, coughing up my guts in town. No one's called me Thomas since my ma died. Which was a few years after – and I haven't seen Matua since – well, let's not get ahead of ourselves. That'll come.

When I look back, that was the last moment before it all went to shit. When we were both just lads, alive and laughing, worried about nothing more than fish in the river. And singing with Matua, it was – when the tune carried on the wind, it was like we were one. Māori and Irish, we both sing for joy and sorrow. We sing because we are alive, we sing to remember the dead, and fuck the English who piss on us both but couldn't carry a tune if the life of their precious Queen depended on it. It's something we share, even whilst the Irish-born soldiers were getting ready to beat the shit out of Matua's cousins down south. And the worst of it was, when I look back now, I realise it was probably us singing so loud that attracted trouble to the spot.

2019

Auckland

Mark liked to move. He liked to move a lot. He also had bright read hair, liked wearing orange, and had green sandals. The impression was of an over-excited traffic light.

"Hey guys! Adele! Ben! So good to see you!"

Adele and Ben looked at each other with a mutual flicker of concern. Mark was, um, one of the more energetic and excitable teens they knew. Mark was the only home schooled teen ever who had been asked not to return to the monthly Jump and Chat meet up at the trampolining centre. It wasn't that he ever meant to cause damage. He wasn't dangerous on purpose. He was just... exuberant and accident-prone. Adele ran her tongue over the small chip in her front tooth that had resulted from the time he tried to triple wham-skadunk her from behind on the smallest trampoline.

"Wow, um, Mark, what a surprise. I thought you were in school now," said Ben.

"Yeah, great to run into you, but don't you have to attend jail on weekday mornings now?" said Adele.

"Ha very ha, you two." Mark dragged a chair over from the next table to join them. He didn't watch what he was doing and the chair leg tipped the table over. A pile of salt, pepper and china fragments littered the floor.

"Oh goodness, Mark." An embarrassed titter. Sheila stood behind him, shaking her head fondly. "You really are a clumsy chops, aren't you, tweetie pie? I should tell you to clean it up but I'm going to give you a big hug instead."

Adele felt her mouth begin to twitch. Sheila's affectionate and demonstrative parenting style was still routinely imitated by the teens at Jump and Chat, even though she and Mark hadn't attended for a few months.

"I'll get a dustpan and brush." Ben leapt to his feet. One thing Adele found ironic about Rosemary was that although their Biblical home school curriculum was very insistent about the differing roles of men and women in the home, she took the pragmatic view that even a dutiful Christian wife might be ill or have a baby now and again, and it was her spiritual duty to ensure her sons were competent at housekeeping before they left home. This also, not incidentally, lightened her own load. Cynthia, by contrast, believed housework was itself an invention of the patriarchy and that it was a liberated woman's duty to ignore as much of it as possible. This meant that Adele learnt to use the washing machine at a very young age, being the only way she could obtain clean clothes. It was one of the reasons the Court Psychologist had suggested she was being exploited and treated as a servant, and possibly ought to be moved to her father's care.

"Aw, thank you, Ben. You're such a sweetheart." Sheila sat down in the chair Mark had moved. "So good to see you two again. We must arrange a play date in the park sometime soon. Maybe picnic lunch."

Adele carefully refrained from pointing out that no one did home school play dates in the park once they had reached double figures. "It's good to see you guys too. But I thought Mark had started school this term."

Sheila sighed a little. "We did experiment with the mainstream schooling option, yes. But it turns out Mark is more of an active learner. He didn't really fit well into the classroom setting. We gave it up after a week. The school was very understanding about letting him go."

"I'm sure they were," Ben replied, in a deadpan tone.

Adele tried to imagine the mess that Mark had made of the classroom during that week, and whether the police had been called.

Sheila squinted at the piece of paper that lay between their empty coffee cups. "So what is this? A home-school project?"

"Yeah." Ben looked up from the floor, where he was knelt sweeping up the mess. "We're going to do a thing about this old box in the attic. Irish family, and coming to the Waikato. At least I am. Adele's just going to nick my sources and copy my work."

"Oh, Waikato history? You'll do New Zealand wars? Wow. Great. That'll be interesting. No one talks about that. But they should." Sheila nodded earnestly in that encouraging home-school-supporter sort of way.

Adele felt a jolt of surprise. "Did you say war?" New Zealand was placid and green. Outside the cities, it seemed mainly to consist of grass and cows. Hard to imagine anyone bothering to go to war over it.

"Yes, war. The Waikato campaign. The bloodiest and most ferocious battles that ever took place in this country happened here." Sheila had a degree in social studies. She knew a lot. Except, it seemed, about effective parenting. "Mark, I am not sure that in an ideal world you should be climbing up on that wall..."

Mark jumped down, landing on the mess that Ben had carefully swept up.

"Did you say Waikato? Are you going to do a field trip?"

Ben groaned at the mess, and ruffled his hair with his fingers in a tired sort of way. He looked quite the film star when he did that.

Adele let her eyes linger discreetly on his arms. Well, not all of them, just the part she could see clearly, his wrists and forearms. There was something there that was not quite right. He was wearing long sleeves, which was odd in itself because the day was quite hot. When he lifted his hand to his face, one sleeve fell down and there were marks, lines, rows of them, all the way down. They looked livid and red. You didn't have to be in school to know what they looked like.

"A field trip? That's a nice idea." Sheila smiled benignly at them all. "You're not too sophisticated for a field trip, are you?"

Ben, realising that his sleeve had fallen, hastily pulled it up. "No, but I can't see how one could visit the whole of the Waikato on a single day trip."

"You'd need to camp. Or go to a motel. Make a road trip of it."

"Road trip! Road trip!" Mark leapt up and started running around the room, in circles. Adele remembered that Sheila was adamantly opposed to the idea of diagnosing children with anything at all, particularly ADHD. Her social studies degree had taught her that society liked to label and medicate anyone who didn't fit the mould. She was insistent that Mark was just a little bit spirited and that it was society that needed to change to accommodate him.

"Why, Sheila. How lovely to see you. And Mark too, of course."

Cynthia and Rosemary were laden with shopping bags and smiles. "He's not in school any more then?"

"No. You would not believe how frighteningly structured and disciplinarian these places are. They want robots not teenagers. If they don't conform, they drug them. Can you believe, the headmaster said he thought Mark would benefit academically and socially from taking Ritalin? I said, over my dead body."

Mark continued to run in circles around the cafe, flapping his arms.

"Your kids were just telling me they were planning a road trip holiday around the region."

Sheila was obviously up to something, since they had said nothing of the kind. Ben and Adele waited to see exactly what.

"It sounds a great way to study their history project. As it happens, I have just bought a campervan. If you liked –"

"Oh!" Cynthia and Rosemary looked at each other with evident excitement. "A few days of outdoor learning –"

"No screens –"

"Doing history through travel, and not in the classroom–"

"I could bring the campervan along and the kids could sleep in it together," suggested Sheila. "Save a bit of money. We adults could have a life of sophistication in motels. Would be an amazing week."

The thought of spending a week sleeping in a campervan with Mark made both Adele and Ben feel a little bit queasy.

"Fabulous," responded Cynthia and Rosemary in unison. Then Rosemary shook her head. "I can't, I'm afraid – bunch of legal meetings."

"Is that still going on?" exclaimed Sheila. "I thought they'd have told him to get lost long ago. That man beat the crap out of you. I can't see why they're even considering giving him share custody now."

"Oh, it's worse than that. He wants full custody, and –"

"He'll never get it." Rosemary folded her arms as if she was a High Court judge. "New Zealand's not that kind of barbaric place."

Cynthia sighed. "You say that, but if you listened to what the other women are going through our support group..."

Adele raised her eyes to the ceiling. That blasted support group. Always carrying placards outside court buildings and making submissions to Government. Sometimes she suspected their life would be much easier if Cynthia hadn't ever fallen in with them and got so passionate about defending her parental rights.

"Well, I worry about the men who lose touch with their kids." Rosemary was clearly in a contrary mood.

"That's nonsense, the courts bend over backwards to please fathers. It's women like me who report domestic violence who get discrimination nowadays."

Adele couldn't keep quiet any longer. "Cynthia, please get off your soapbox."

Cynthia didn't seem to hear. "I mean it, Rosemary. Have you seen the latest reports from the United Nations?"

This was an awkward subject, because Rosemary belonged to the segment of the Christian community who thinks that global organisations such as the U.N. and Amnesty International are partnering with the Devil. Fortunately, Sheila interrupted.

"Sounds like you need a holiday then.Anyway, this is exactly the sort of evidence the courts will need."

Adele and Ben looked at each other resignedly and mouthed the inevitable words as Sheila spoke them. "Great opportunity for socialisation."

"Well." Cynthia thought for moment, then laughed. "Oh, screw it. I'm fed up with doing what my lawyer wants. Yes, why not? It's only a week. What could go wrong?"

Great, Adele thought sarcastically to herself, we are going to spend a week babysitting Mark and looking at cows. Cynthia will probably rabbit on about how I should be proud to be Māori, and I will want to kill her. Rosemary will definitely find a river and try to baptise me on the sly. But at least it will be a break from the sodding social workers and court psychologists asking me why I don't have any friends.

She glanced across at Ben. Yes, the field trip was a good idea. With a bit of luck, if they were all squashed up in a campervan together someone else might notice those worrying cuts on his arms.

1862

Port Waikato

The ritual of thanksgiving for the catch was Matua's job. Thomas didn't join in. That way it was easier. No sins of idol worship to bring to Father Murphy's dark and tobacco-scented confessional booth on a Saturday night.

Now you might wonder why I write about myself when I was young as *he*. It's simply easier, when I'm looking back over fifty years or more. The boy that I was and the man I became both seem distant and unclear. Wavering in the heat of my memory like a puff of smoke from the cannon that practiced north of us in those simple days. He's the boy, laughing with his friend. Me, I'm the old man who is puffing out his last breaths and scratching with my best copperplate on cheap notepad. Best to keep it separate, like the Hail Mary Thomas said in church and the karakia he listened to on the boat. No point in worrying the old man, although it was true Father Murphy took a more pragmatic view of these things than his Anglican colleagues. Mr James was an Anglican, and great friends with Reverend Simpson, the Anglican minister who had recently come out to begin missionary activities in the area.

Father Murphy did not hold with too much missionising. He had been known to point out drunkenly that for the way these missionary Protestants carried on about the sinful Māori, you would think that Our Lord Jesus himself had been born a respectably baptised Christian, instead of a dark-skinned heathen Jew. He would offer anyone the chance of a bottle of whisky if they could find a verse in the Bible that proved otherwise. Mr Simpson and Mr James avoided alcohol as if it were a fast route to hell. After a few such conversations, they avoided Father Murphy too.

Matua whistled. "You know what? I forgot to piss on the poraka before we took it out. That's bad luck. Those mudfish could be cursed."

Thomas' heart sank. There'd been a time when curses were a distant threat. But that was before the taiaha disappeared.

He lunged at the precious catch. "You are not pissing on them now. Nor throwing them back."

Matua flicked him aside, with ease. "Get off me, white boy. What are you going to do, call Governor Grey?"

Thomas came at him again. Matua knocked him a second time, harder now. He fell downwards. Common sense told him he would lose. Like all his Māori classmates, Matua spent hours practicing rongo mamau, traditional wrestling. But the idea of letting his friend piss on the fish for dinner revolted him.

"You can't do that," he snarled through a mouthful of sand. "I don't care what your tohunga says. My tohunga says it is disgusting."

Matua hesitated for a moment. "Your Priest says you can't pee on fish?"

"Yeah. It's a Catholic rule. The fish is a Christian symbol so if I piss on it it's like being disrespectful to our Lord. I'll go to hell if I let you do it. I've got to fight you to the death." Thomas crossed his fingers discreetly, and made a mental note to confess the fib.

Matua considered the situation, and shrugged. "I'll fight you, then." He pushed Thomas' chin backwards, and rested a heavy foot on his stomach. "If you're sure."

The air escaping from Thomas' belly made a loud fart. Both of them yelped with laughter. Matua waved his spare arm in front of his nose. "What the hell did you have for breakfast this morning? Rotten eggs?"

Thomas knew it was a sign he'd been forgiven. He sprawled out on the sand. Matua frowned. "Don't think I've changed my mind. I'm still going to piss on the fish. And we're going to do the blood ritual properly. Give me one."

There was no point in arguing. The rituals were the rituals, and that's how it was. Once, when they were younger, Matua might have been persuaded. But then since his brother sold the family taiaha, the pressure on the Waikato from the north had been unrelenting. Now, when it came to upholding tradition, he was rigid. As if he could singlehandedly hold back the tide of bad luck that was surely about to engulf his hapu by passionate adherence to the ancestors' ways. You might as well argue with the sea or the tides.

Thomas scrambled to his feet, dusting down the sand and soil from his bare legs. There were bruises, as if Matua had wanted to remind him yet again that he was still the boss, no matter how many Pākehā soldiers were surging into the district. He took a small, slimy black wetfish and handed it over nervously. It was still wriggling. Helplessly, like he'd been on the sand a few minutes before. The closer they came to war, the harsher it seemed Matua was.

With a sudden movement, Matua broke the fish's head off. Blood spurted up, into their faces. "Don't swallow it!" He shouted in alarm. Thomas shook his head. He knew already that anything to do with fishing was tapu, and you must not eat or drink until the sacred work time was over. Sometimes when they were on the water he almost cried with thirst, but he knew if he weakened and drank even a drop of river water Matua would never trust him to come on the boat again. Now he watched as Matua sprinkled the bright fish blood over the net. "Can you get a stake? We need to spear the fish and leave it as an offering for the spirits."

Thomas, his eyes blurry with dried blood, made his way

up the beach. A piece of driftwood caught his eye. Some jagged stones lay beside it. Strange shapes. The driftwood was perfect for what they needed, but those stones caught his eye. They were like the ones he had seen in Auckland once, when he and his father had been visiting a stonemason about his brother's grave.

"Ah, these?" The stonemason had said, with a smile, keen to break away from the dismal task of discussing budget gravestone options for an Irish settler child who had inconveniently chosen the costly option of dying just as they had reached land. "These are what the scientific folk are calling fossils. They say they're older than Creation. All the rage." He talked for a few minutes, about science and the Bible and geological maps that suggested Britain was lying flat on its side. The fossils were dead animals, he explained. Just really, really old ones. Thomas found that idea strangely comforting. Perhaps his brother would turn into a fossil too.

"Look!" Thomas ran back down the beach. "These are really valuable."

Matua took the driftwood and speared the fish, murmuring a karakia. He took the stones.

"Why? What are they?"

Thomas was bursting with pride. "The Bible says the world was created in seven days but that's wrong. The man in Auckland explained it. These fossils show how, we used to be fish all of us. Living in the sea. Then we grew legs and came to land."

Matua nodded thoughtfully. "Yes, that could work with our tradition, I suppose. When Rangi and Papa had - "

Thomas snickered. "I know the story, even if you aren't supposed to tell me. They were rutting with each other in the sky with their kids between them. I know."

Matua hesitated, then gave a crafty smile. "I'm not saying yes or no. And I'm not saying that they created the world, and there was the Great War between heaven and earth, the fish and the reptiles sought shelter in the land and the sea, but we don't know what order that happened. But what I'm saying, if it did happen like that, it would mean the fossils were true. Cool."

"And we can sell them. For lots. I can get new shoes."

Matua smiled. "Yes. But you know what? No matter how many fossils you find, no matter how much money you tell me we're going to make, I'm still going to piss on that fish."

Thomas shrugged. Worse things happened at sea.

Just as Matua was about to lower his pants, a shadow fell over them, sharp-edged and sinister, like the stones that had been thrown at them a few minutes earlier. They had been followed, spied upon. Matua whirled around, buttoning his breeches. "What? Sir?"

Thomas was not quick enough. He turned, to see a pair of thin lips, and a cold stare. Then there was the crash of Mr James's staff to the back of his head.

2019

Mangere Village

So let's get this factoid straight, I'm not a pussy. I know how to use a blade in a fight. Maybe I wouldn't have gone that way if I'd stayed at home, but by about my seventeenth foster placement I was over being gentle and nice and waiting for the world to like me.

Still, I'm not the kinda guy who gets a kick out of it. Just because you know how to slice off a fingertip and persuade the kid to make out it was an accident, doesn't mean you're the kind of sick bastard who'll do it for fun.

So I didn't want to hurt anyone. Not anyone at the protest, anyway. And I'm not a fool. I knew how it would look. Yeah, so the press onsite seemed pretty onto it, but you know how these things can turn overnight. *Murderous Protestors! Respectable visitor to building site bludgeoned to death by Ihumātao thugs.* We'd lose the public relations argument overnight. Might as well pack up and go home.

But there he was, that bastard. And I tell you, he had no right to be alive. What's worse, every day that he lived he'd have the chance to do to others the kind of sick stunts he pulled on me.

I was meant to be on frontline duty that morning. Sorry, yeah, I forgot you don't know all the terms. Frontline was where eight or nine of us sat, right up by the police. We sang and kicked ideas around, but mainly we just did the mahi of holding them back. Later, when things settled a bit, we got to be in a tent, protected from the rain, and cops stood back. But this was the early days. They still thought a bit of professional aggro and we'd get scared and go home. So they kept trying to drive their trucks through, and when we wouldn't move to let them, they had a line of blue right up against our chairs.

It was hard mahi, I'm telling you. But I didn't mind that, sitting tight and giving anyone who tried to move me lip, that's what a life in care had prepped me for. No, the reason I didn't show up to duty that morning, asked my sis to deal instead, it was this. The same routine every day, when you showed up. Reminder to write your next of kin and their mobile number on your arm. Reminder of your rights, what you do and don't do down the cop shop, or in the paddy wagon.

One blonde bro got upset hearing that term, said it was anti Irish. I never knew that before, just like I didn't know it was wrong to call a stingy ass a Jew. Yeah, I learnt a lot sitting up there on the front lines, all the cultures squashed up chatting together. Weird. We'd never have got so close to each other if it wasn't for the police. Anyway, none of that was the problem. We were treated good, brought cups of tea and food. If we needed a piss there was always someone ready who could take our place.

No, the problem was a promise. Now there's promises and promises. The promise you give to your social worker that you'll try to do better? Nah. You only say that so she'll get fed up chewing you out and go away. Promise to Thin-Lips, that you'll keep his nasty work quiet, never let it out? Yeah nah, you'll keep that. But only cause you're bricking yourself for what'll happen if you don't.

But this was, yeah I'm not religious, but Ihumātao, it was like a sacred place, you know. Holy land, something like that. Like they say in Israel, not that I've ever been. The thing is, the kaumātua used to say our ancestors were all around, supporting us, like a sort of invisible cloud. I dunno if it was true or not. But I'm telling you, nights in the fog, it was spooky. Like we weren't alone. Like the sea and the river and a whole load of dead people, yeah, it wasn't hard to believe they'd turned up to support the kaupapa too.

Careful now, don't take me for one of those new agey types. Cause there were a lot of them too. They buzzed around us like flies on a shit, tried to make believe like us sitting out freezing our arses in a field was the beginning of some Grand Global Aquarian Rainbow Era. I remember one night there was this greenie chick, she'd done oil and gas exploration protests too. Reckoned she knew a lot, liked to hear herself talk. You know the type. Anyway, she came up to where we were sitting by the bonfire, and was all "Oh, not much happening here, I can see you're all feeling low tonight, we're holding lots of negative energy, let me give you some crystals." She didn't realise the reason we were quiet is we were all stoned off our tits.

And the problem is with that kinda fake spiritual chit-chat, it kinda drives the other underground. Because there was a strong kinda sense to the place, a mana of its own if you like. You'd look up at the stars at night, and it felt the Milky Way was closer than ever before. Sorta still and buzzing at once. You sorta knew you were in the right place, and doing what you were supposed to do. Like the stars themselves were going, *shot bro, you're doing great, stand your ground*. And no, it wasn't just the effect of the weed.

Prolly sounds daft to you. Especially if you're Pākehā and don't buy into any of our culture and think it's all superstitious fairy tales, like the story about the lost taiaha. Straight up, sometimes I think the same way too. But yeah nah, I didn't want to blaspheme or lie to the whānau. Not with the whole whakapapa listening.

And this was the thing. Frontline was run by a big bro, imposing. I dunno how old he was. All I know, he had lots of energy and even more mana, so when you looked at him, he seemed sort of old and young at once. His feet were bare, half the time, like he didn't even feel the cold.

And he'd ask us the same question at the start of every shift. It was this. Are you prepared to go to jail to protect this land? And are you prepared not to resist, and not answer violence with violence?

I could answer the first with a yes. I wanted to answer the second the same way. It was vital, I got it, that we didn't look like extras from *Once Were Warriors*. If we're going to win this PR round, the last thing we can afford to do is scare the Pakeha. But all I could do was mumble. I couldn't promise non-violence. Not with Thin-Lips around.

Late Holocene River Time

Aii. The whitebait roams free, and so do I.

I am the river of stars at which you gaped, crossing the skies above Ihumātao. But I'm also the water running clouded and pitiful by the campfires, the broken strands of the Oruarangi river. Further south, I become myself more clearly. They toss me through a hydroelectric dam, but I thrash and survive. I throw myself off mountains and flow with the eels through polluted oily waters. I am the great god Waikato.

If I appear verbose, so be it. Water is like that. It runs wherever it finds a course. I travel through time. I am the original story. I write myself on the bare rock pages of land. I let them flow under me, the way Pākehā paper surges and ripples and dives under the steady pen. As Rangi and Papa lay, so do I and the riverbed: the foreshore, and the seafloor. I foreplay in the wetlands and undress in the high angular mountains. My shallow ripples gush into the salty, waiting, open sea. Thou art my lover, Land. And I am your rider. I trickle down your crevices, leaving you deepened and crushed.

No one remembers the time of their birth. If Maui indeed pulled us all up from Tangaroa's lair, I do not recall, any more than being carved out of rock by the Great Ice of the Pleistocene. When Kupe came though, now that was a different, memorable, story. The puny Godboy, proudly riding his waka like a toy. Like a London urchin, peddling his tricycle. Hey, he was barely off his mother's tit, just a few years old, paddling himself with chubby hands and grazed knees. Changing the land as he went, like a kohanga reo kid knocking over blocks and falling over the grammar of his tupuna today. The only reason you modern ones remember him as the Great Explorer is that you are even smaller and sillier than he.

I knew Kupe was trouble, and I tried to drive him off. I took his canoe and I threw it high, up into the waves. My great eels *nga tuna nui* thrashed and bit at its wooden hull. "Give it back to us," they whispered. "Go home to Hawaikii where you belong."But he persisted. "This is a country for people," he told us, clinging onto his paddle while we mercilessly bashed his boat against the rocks. "I want my family to live here." No one can beat the power of a river, but even a river has to give way in the end and merge silently into the saltiness of sea. Sulky, I let him have his boat and sail away. "You may become tangata whenua," I catcalled. "But you will never own me or the sea."

Now Hape, Hape was a different netful of fish. Hape the turtle rider, solitary crosser of oceans, founder of Ihumātao. The man with a dragging leg. The boy who could not forgive. When Hape came I did not have to beat him down. He was already broken, a forsaken man. His brothers built a mud wall cottage around him whilst he slept, blocking out the light so he would not wake until they had all left Hawaiiki. For who would want to travel to mountainous cold Aotearoa with a cripple?

Kupe, Maui, these are household words. Not so with the story of Hape and the turtle that brought him from Hawaiiki. No one these days has time for Hape stories. Unless they're holding back the police lines with nothing but their sore bums to protect them, shivering for lonely hours in their plastic chairs on the front line.

2018

Port Waikato

"Oh, for goodness sake, Cynthia, you can't head back to Auckland now. We've only just started our trip."

"I have to. They've fixed a Family Group Conference." Cynthia flapped her hands despairingly.

"Who have?"

"Oranga Tamariki. CYFS. The Ministry. Whatever you call them these days."

"What'll they do if you don't turn up? Take Adele into care?" Rosemary bellowed scornfully. "You're a good mother. They know that. Just text them and say you'll be back in a week."

Adele rolled her eyes at the ceiling. These conversations had been going on for so long she had almost forgotten the time when Cynthia wasn't a stressed out wreck. Sometimes she thought she might just volunteer to go to school, if it stopped the whole mess. But she suspected that wouldn't satisfy her dad. He'd just complain about something else.

"Travel Scrabble?" Ben suggested, with a bright changing-the-subject smile. "Come on, I haven't beaten anyone for at least an hour or two."

"Now come on, Mark, it's time for Hebrew study." Sheila poked her head around the campervan door. "Go sit down." She scrambled past their baggage to the campervan table, and laid down a printed sheet. "You need to do it before dinner."

Mark shook his head. "Don't wanna. Not on holiday."

"Oh, sweetie. Do you want to be the only teen boy in the synagogue who hasn't had a barmitzvah?"

Mark shook his head. "Don't care."

"All those presents. Money and sweets." Sheila pleaded.

Mark shrugged. "Not on holiday."

That was the thing about caravanning on a roadtrip, Adela thought, you found out all sorts of extraordinary things about people. Mark and Sheila were Jewish. Who knew? Not her. Like she hadn't known she snored until Mark threw a pillow at her at three a.m.

"All right," Sheila suggested with a sigh, "if you really don't want to, why not go for a nice walk first and burn off some energy. We can try again later."

Ben and Adele looked at each other resignedly. No one directly asked them, but they knew the Travel Scrabble feud would have to wait. Mark wasn't exactly safe on his own.

They were staying in Port Waikato. It was a small town. The kind of place where nothing happened, and nobody came and nobody left, except for six weeks in the summer. Now it was winter and even the holiday park was closed. Kura kaupapa and kohanga reo seemed to be the only community buildings. An irritating quiet ache settled on Adele when she looked at them, like it'd maybe been a mistake to refuse when Cynthia offered to get her a tutor in Māori.

"I want to go swimming," Mark announced, as soon as they were out of the campervan. Ben pointed out they had no togs. Mark, who could be quite sharp when he wanted to get his own way, suggested they swim in their undies and go commando on the way home.

"But no towels," moaned Ben. "We'll freeze."

Adele looked at him sharply. It wasn't that cold. In fact, they'd run themselves into such a sweat earlier that they'd ended up rubbing chilled Coke cans from the campsite vending machine against their cheeks to cool down. The real reason, she suspected, was that Ben didn't want to go swimming was that he didn't want to get undressed and show anyone his arms. But Ben lucked out, because when they went to ask directions for where it was safe to swim, the shopkeeper told them they'd have to go inland. Not even the river was safe.

Mark gave a howl. "You would say that."

Adela changed the subject deftly. "Nice old store building, this."

"Yes." The elderly gentleman beamed with familial pride.

"Yeah, be a shame if anything happened to it," shouted Mark. "Because there was nowhere we could swim."

The storeowner's friendly smile dissolved into a horrified scowl.

"Sorry, don't mind him," gabbled Ben. "He's just a bit -" He stopped, trying to think of an appropriate word that would not leave Mark in tears.

"- Enthusiastic," Adele smiled reassuringly. "He's right, though, it is nice."

The storekeeper nodded.

"My family's been traders here since the Port was founded. Ships would come in on their way to Manukau harbour further north. We sold a bit of everything, back then. Only shop for miles. Of course now it's mainly ice creams and bucket-and-spade trade for the tourists."

Mark groaned loudly. It was a hot day and they'd been doing history with Sheila all morning. "OK, so no beach swim. Can we dip in the river?"

"Not really, no. Current's bad there too. Even boats can be tricky. Are you going across to the East Coast? I'd wait to swim there." The guy winked.

"No. We're on a road trip following the Waikato. Sort of a history project and holiday mixed up."

"Sounds great. Wish I'd done stuff like that at school when I was young."

Adela and Ben glanced at each other and held their

tongues. Home education was not something you discussed with strangers if you didn't want to get a lecture along the lines of "butwhataboutdoingyourexams" and socialisation. Adela expected Mark to blurt out the truth, but even he seemed to have absorbed that basic rule. People don't understand home educated kids, so never tell them you are one until you have to.

"Are you all at school together?"

"Yes." Ben spoke firmly. That was what Jesus was for, after all, forgiving sins like slander and lies. Anyway, he reasoned to himself, it was essentially true. School was on this road trip, and that is where they were now.

"You've got a Jewish name," Mark unexpectedly announced to the shopkeeper, looking at the liquor licence behind the counter. "Curren. My dad says that's Cohen for people who don't want to say they're Jews."

The shopkeeper opened his mouth, then shut it again.

"I go to Hebrew School," Mark continued, not waiting for a reply. "But only on Sundays." He considered. "Actually, I don't go any more. The rabbi says I am, incorrigible." He giggled. "You know what the Talmud says? You can be counted as a man for the purposes of a minyan, if you have more than ten pubes. And guess what?" He started to pull at his surfer shorts.

Adele and Ben leapt on him with practised speed and dragged him outside.

So now they were walking on the beach. Sheila, who turned out to be quite good at teaching stuff when she wasn't running around after Mark, had told them that some of the earliest fossil discoveries in New Zealand had been made in Port Waikato. Looking at the jagged broken cliffs running at diagonals into the sea, that made sense.

"I want to take some photos." Adele unslung her mother's camera from her neck. "Look at that black rock. The reflections." They danced into the sea the way her mother described the world looking when she had been young and childfree enough to drop tabs on a weekend. *You know, Adele*, she would confide over a glass of wine, *what I learnt from all that experimenting was that actually most of the best things in life are natural. You don't need to go off and fry your brain to find fun. It's out here, in the real world. Life is wonderful enough.* That was after the first glass. After the second or third, she would giggle a bit and admit, that actually, there was a buzz you got from some substances that nothing, not even sex, could emulate – definitely not your dad, at least – and that when Adele was old enough they'd go mushroom hunting together. *But not whilst your brain's still developing, all right?* If only her dad didn't keep making out her mum was a drugged up wreck who shouldn't have charge of a goldfish.

Mark splashed Ben, who forgot he was too sophisticated to play and splashed him back. They pranced off down the beach like dogs that were being let off the leash by local pet-owners. Adela had meant to take photographs of the seascape, but their puppyish movements impelled her to record them. A timeless quality to the scene, young men slapping each other on the back and throwing water around on a sunny day at the beach. Must have been happening for centuries here. Since Port Waikato was founded, maybe before.

Time was just an illusion, Rosemary always said. *Once,* she'd giggled after several glasses of wine, *she'd taken a tab on the beach and the magic mushrooms were ten times stronger than the usual type, or maybe she'd just taken ten times as much,* Adele couldn't remember. Anyway, the point was illusory nature of time.

Rosemary had dissolved into the sea and became a butterfly. She had been a butterfly for ages, flew up to the place where the stars turned into the beginning of time and beyond, and she became a wondrous being of light, just like everyone else. It was all great until she came down to Earth again and found the maggoty underneaths of the world where nasty curling creatures waved giant antennae at her. Yeah, that would give her social worker a heart attack if she talked about it. Probably take her away on the spot, no matter that Rosemary hadn't touched a hallucinogen for twenty years.

Adele looked down at the camera. Low power. Damn. Still, there was probably enough juice left to take a few snaps. She swung around, letting the lens whirr as she moved. A maggot moved at the bottom of the cliff. No, that was wrong, you couldn't see an insect from that far away. Everything was still now, anyway. She squinted carefully, then took a final shot. The photo steady and clear, like the hot windless day.

Then she saw him again. The maggot. But not in front of her, this time, just on the digital reading of the photograph. A smudge, it seemed at first, perhaps a raindrop on the lens. By the bottom of the cliffs, behind where Mark and Ben whooped and flapped their arms. She zoomed in, curious as to what had caused the imperfection. If it was an imperfection, though, it was a human one: a man. Standing at the edge of the cliff, watching them it seemed. But surely he wasn't, because there was nothing interesting to watch. He must have been looking at the sea, or the sky. And how had he got into the photograph, when she had checked so carefully that the beach in front of them was clear?

Mark bounced up to her, his face shining with exuberance and seawater. "Did you have fun?" He giggled. "I offered to show Ben I had more than ten pubes, but he didn't want to see."

Adela looked down the beach. No. There was definitely nobody there.

1862

Port Waikato

The horse gave a fruity belch, and lurched to the left. Thomas lost his balance, and jolted forward. Another cuff to the head. Port Waikato was receding into the distance behind them. Thomas gulped, and tried not to cry.

As he fell, he'd accidentally looked across at Matua, despite Mr James's firm instructions that for the whole of the journey they were not to speak to each other and only look ahead. Mr James seemed to take great pleasure in making sure that whenever he had to strike Thomas, it was always in the same place on the head that he had knocked him out the day before. And every time he looked at Thomas, he gave a nasty little snigger, the way he had when he'd spoken sarcastically about *the love between two young men*. Thomas was still trying to work out what all that meant. He was an innocent young lad, you see. Not like the larrikans you meet in the street these days who'll offer you a blowjob for sixpence, the second word gets around town you might be one of those.

At least, Thomas thought, the blow wasn't hard. Not like the one yesterday on the river shore. He had been halfway back to the south side of the Waikato estuary before he came to. Matua rowed the boat whilst Mr James sat regally in the front seat, puffing tobacco smoke at them both, a revolver in his hand. The smoke had sickening stench, made worse by the fish entrails that had sprayed all over all the boat and were rapidly rotting in the afternoon sun.

Thomas tried to get up, but Mr James, stroked the revolver and pushed a casual foot into his chest.

"Stay there. You've been concussed. I don't want you falling overboard. Not until you have both received adequate punishment."

Thomas was not sure what they'd done but he could hear in Mr James's voice that it was bad. He tried to think, but his head was fuzzy. Yes, they'd taken out the boat on a day when fishing was regarded as unlucky by the natives, but that was hardly something that would concern the likes of Mr James. They'd fought, a little, but again, Mr James practically encouraged that amongst the schoolchildren. There was the business of the fossil stones, he supposed. But it couldn't be that. That was knowledge, and Mr James was a schoolteacher.

But it was the fossils. Mr James, it turned out, did not like all forms of knowledge. Nor did the Reverend Simpson, to whose squat white wooden board rectory the boys were immediately taken by horse and cart when the exhausted Matua had pulled the boat ashore.

"I have of course beaten them both soundly already," Mr James told the Reverend, on arrival at the white-gabled cottage adjoining the church. This was true: they had both been required to make a detour to the schoolhouse, drop their breeches and receive twelve strokes of the cane apiece for the devilish manner in which they were promulgating demonic theories. It was a golden rule amongst the schoolchildren never to give the schoolmaster the satisfaction of showing pain or fear, but Thomas could not hold back a few weak wails. Matua, of course, was as silent as a stone.

"Well yes, I am sure you have done your educational duty. But I fear for your tender mindedness, James. To be honest I doubt a single beating will be enough to purge the sin." The Reverend stood on his freshly-scrubbed front step. He'd obviously been waiting a while for them. But how could he have known? wondered Thomas.

The thick-walled vicarage was unusual in Port Waikato. The Reverend's predecessor had supervised the construction himself. A wise man builds his house on rock, he reminded anyone who would listen. Unfortunately, his knowledge of the Bible was not matched by his wisdom in the niceties of colonial house building. Most pioneers felled trees and made log cabins, then gradually replaced them with pine boards when time and resources allowed. He'd insisted on a traditional Cotswolds cob cottage, with thatched roof. Mud was easy enough to find, but the reeds that grew in the Waikato did not have the same tenacious quality as English straw. They fell off the roof in drifts and rotted in sweet-smelling piles on the gravel paths. Sweeping them up was a fulltime job. Since the Reverend had been waiting a while, he wore a gentle dusting of dried kakaho. The effect, Thomas thought, was of a very tidy and angular scarecrow. Unmoving and patient, but somehow unnerving. As if they were thieving birds, and the house itself was trying to warn them off.

The Reverend ushered them into his study. Books lined the walls. Thomas liked reading in small doses, but these leather covered tomes seemed to wear an intimidating frown, like the gargoyles on Dublin cathedral. "Stand there, boys. By the fireplace." He cracked his knuckles like a whip. "Stay still. Don't speak, and don't make a run for it. I am locking the door and the garden boy has been warned to stop you if you try to escape. Mr James and I need to talk in private."

Thomas heard the muttered voices in the hallway. He could not help shaking and he thought he might wet himself. That often happened after a beating at school. He wondered how it was that Matua managed to shrug it off, as though he didn't feel a thing.

Matua didn't speak. He breathed heavily – through his nose – and stared at the door. Impossible to tell whether he was breathing deeply because he wanted to keep calm, or because he simply didn't care.

They seemed to have waited forever, when the door opened. Both Mr James and Reverend Simpson seemed quite jolly now, as if this was all an excellent afternoon's fun.

"My father won't like this." Matua's voice, shaking slightly. "He'll want to come and have a word."

Reverend Simpson laughed. "It's Matua, isn't it? Your father's a powerful man in this area. Or at least he was, before the arrival of the soldiers. General Cameron has a different view, thank heaven, of the Māori problem than the weaselly-minded governors. There is European muscle here now, and I expect he'll be minded to use it."

He approached Matua and stared hard, triumphantly. Matua looked him back, levelly and straight in the eye. Thomas hoped that Reverend Simpson was new enough to New Zealand that he did not know that that was a signal of disrespect. Perhaps he did. He came closer, bowed his head and unexpectedly snapped his teeth. Matua flinched.

"Not so brave now, are you? We're going to make an example of you, Matua. All the area knows how important your father is and all the area knows that he doesn't want the Māori people Christened. Your father has been one of the biggest obstacles to the Lord's work in this region."

He took hold of Matua's ear and squeezed slightly. Thomas flinched, as though the ear was his own. Once they'd fallen on the ground whilst wrestling, and for a second Matua had looked into his eyes and stretched out a hand. He'd touched Thomas' earlobe gently, then withdrawn awkwardly when the other boy did not respond.

"You will be baptised as your mother wishes. And you will go with Mr James to his new boarding school for Anglican Māori. What have you to say to that?"

Matua smacked his lips. A globule of spit landed on the polished wood.

Reverend Simpson's voice was soft and clear. "Don't do that again, or you will be licking up worse than that off my floor."

Matua swayed slightly, the way the reeds did in the wetlands. But his voice was steady. "I won't go."

"Yes, Matua, you will. Because if not I will order your father arrested and sent to Auckland prison for sedition."

"True," broke in Mr James. "Your father has been very foolish for a while. This is frontier country, and the army is on the move."

Reverend Simpson lowered his voice even further. Now it was so quiet Thomas had to strain to hear. "Do you know what the Auckland prison is like for Māori these days, boy? Much worse than a nice spell at boarding school."

Matua bit his lip, and did not reply. Outside, a tui chattered. It hurt to turn his head, but when he did so Thomas saw it sucking contentedly on a pohutakawa branch. Just like a normal day. Two hours ago, it was. Now he was dizzy and tired, and in the middle of a bad dream.

There was silence. They were waiting for Matua to speak, Thomas supposed. Or perhaps they were just waiting out for him to realise he wasn't going to, that he was trapped in a snare like one of those new foreign rabbits, and there wasn't any point in making trouble for himself by answering back.

Reverend Simpson exhaled, slowly. "I think the simple native understands his predicament. Good." With an air of moving on two men looked across at Thomas.

"I suppose you are wondering what your punishment will be, Thomas?" Mr James asked in a jocular tone, the way a cat might joke with a mouse, or a dog with a particularly juicy bone. "You were always a conniving type. I noticed your craftiness when we played chess with your sister. I should, to be honest, be much angrier with you than I am. Boys will experiment, with - forbidden fruit, after all. I did much the same when I was young."

He came closer, and ruffled Thomas' hair affectionately. Thomas had never wanted to be touched by anyone less. There are no snakes in Ireland or New Zealand, but on the boat they'd stopped at Morocco. A man had come aboard with a cobra in a basket. For a farthing, you could have it laid around your neck and shudder at the touch of its scaly hide. That was how it felt, to be stroked by Mr James. Only that cobra had been defanged, its venom ducts cut. It only looked fearsome. The opposite was true of mild, bespectacled, thin-lipped Mr James.

"The difficulty is that you are Catholic. We cannot simply hand you back to your church. Confession makes it too easy to get away with sin. That drunken old fool would have you repeat a few Pater Nostras and that would be the end of it. Clearly you are the ringleader in this little escapade and your dissolute priest is incapable of restraining you. For the sake of King and Country we can no longer allow you live freely in Port Waikato without putting the morality of our whole community at risk."

Reverend Simpson coughed a little. "It is my view that the Anglican Church here has been far too liberal in its dealings with Catholics. A blasphemy trial would send a clear message that this colony will no longer tolerant criminal scum." He sat at his oaken study desk down with an air of having made a wise decision.

Mr James held Thomas's hand. It was a strange thing to do, in the circumstances, Thomas though, as if he was trying to court me.

"But I am fond of you, Thomas," said Mr James, "I think you are not beyond redemption yet. Prison would harden you, bring you into contact with all the worst influences. You would be, how do I put it, tasty untouched fruit for the corrupt, and I do not want that to happen to you. Instead you could benefit from spending more time with me. And I would enjoy that, I think. In my hands you could be opened like a flower, instead of brutally cracked like an egg."

Reverend Simpson laughed sardonically.

Mr James went on, his voice as soft as butter. "So we have agreed we are going to give you a final chance. Only Māori students are permitted at the boarding school but I have room in my accommodation to house a single student. I shall tutor you myself in the traditions of, ahem, the Greeks, and if all goes well you will be permitted to attend school with the other students. I shall explain to your father that I am arranging for you to stay with me there, given the urgent need to –" He stroked Thomas's cheek for a moment. Thomas flinched. But what was there to be afraid of. Mr James was being kind to him. "– tenderly reform your character."

Reverend Simpson picked up a pen. "I am writing a letter to make appropriate arrangements now. You leave tonight. Until then I will make arrangements for you to be locked in the coalshed."

"But our families." Thomas burst out. "We need to say goodbye."

Mr James looked at him fondly. "So young. So untouched."

Reverend Simpson regarded them both with a lizard-like stare. "I do not intend to give the paddies or the natives any opportunity to cause trouble before you go. The word has already been put out that you have been diagnosed with an infectious disease, and that I have kindly kept you here in quarantine. By the time the truth is told to your families, you will both be hundreds of miles away."

Thomas gave a short sob.

"Oh, spare me your tears. You won't find much sympathy if you start crying at school."

Thomas tried to stop crying, but he couldn't. Undignified, sniffling tears, just the kind that in the classroom would guarantee a beating. There was an ominous pause, and then Mr James raised his hand.

Instantly, Matua lunged forward and bit him, hard on

the arm. Now it was the teacher's turn to howl.

"You little savage! How dare you!" Matua clamped his jaws with the strength of an eel. Mr James shook his arm uselessly and roared. Thomas couldn't imagine how his friend could dare, or what the point of such resistance could be. There was an undignified scuffle that ultimately resulted in Matua's head being stuffed into a coal sack, and his hands and feet hog-tied.

The Reverend sank into an armchair and mopped his sweating forehead. His shirt was torn, exposing tufts of grey chest hair. No wonder he's uncomfortable about the theory of ape ancestry, Thomas thought. Everyone waited for Mr James to start thrashing the younger boy again, but he seemed to have forgotten all about that.

"I'll make you pay," the teacher snarled into the coal sack, rubbing his bleeding arm. "But not until we've arrived at school." He opened the study window. The scratchy sound of kakaho reed being raked over river sediment gravel floated into the room. "Boy. Leave that for now, would you? I have a couple of packages that need to be delivered to the coalshed."

The Reverend coughed, gathering his breath. He gave Thomas and the coalsack a withering stare. "Nasty little creatures, both of you. What they really need, James, is a reformatory where they'd get some real discipline. " He gazed out of the window towards the distant water, as though expecting a fully-kitted-out reformatory to arrive and be unloaded on the wharf any moment. "So poor, kind Mr James will just have to be given a free hand to reform you on his own."

"And Matua." Mr James knelt down closer to the hog-tied sack, and spoke with the air of producing a cherished trump card. "Do you think I am such a fool, as not to notice how you bit me to stop me walloping Thomas. Truly, love between young men is a beautiful thing." He snickered. "In view of your deep feelings, I'll let him be for now. But don't think if you mess me around a second time, he will survive unscathed. Tomorrow morning we'll let you out of that sack, and you'll run and fetch and carry just as if you were a beaten dog. I'll brand your little friend Thomas on his bare behind, inside and out, if you step out of line again."

2019

Mangere Village

Let's get real. It didn't matter if I swore to non-violence or not. I couldn't have jumped up and bashed Thin-Lips anyway. Because the old maggot was surrounded by police and bureaucrats. Council, mostly. You could tell by their lanyards and nervous expressions. Probably some from the building company. They were strolling around, strutting their stuff like they'd already run. And a few senior police officers. You could tell they were senior 'cause unlike the rest they weren't all bundled up in extra layers and gloves. Like they knew it wouldn't be their job to hold protesters back in the cold.

They were all having some meeting behind the crash fence. Waving bits of paper around. Couldn't tell what they were up to. But he was surrounded. Safe as if he's been in a hornet's nest. No way could I get near him. Not even enough to do a bit of damage before I was dragged away. Anyway, we were supposed to be paying attention to the morning meeting.

It was all pretty standard stuff. A didgeridoo had arrived from a parallel protest in Oz. Apparently there's a group who're protesting about some sacred tree. Same kinda jaunt. Anyway, we play protest pen pal ping-pong: they send us their stuff and we send ours back. Shoulda asked them to send it all by boomerang, save a bit on postage. Same with those bros in Hawaii who want to stop the telescope. We get stuff from them too. And that oil pipeline in Dakota, or wherever it is. All over the world, same mix of kids and kaumātua, standing up to the bosses. It was kinda nice. Like we belonged, and weren't just a group of no-good-drop-outs getting wrecked on weed in a field.

Some posh chick from the North Shore got up and wanted us to organise a camp school. Her kids were on school strike for Ihumātao, she said, to cheers. But they needed educational nourishment, mustn't just run wild in the camp. Fewer cheers. She wondered if parents might like to set up a teaching rota and erect a special tent so her precious darlings didn't get left behind. My sis looked at me and made gagging sounds.

Whilst the camp coordinator tried to shut her up, I noticed this gorgeous girl with the cutest eyes in front of me. I'd seen her earlier, when she was trying to make the coffee urn work in the breakfast tent. Only then she was all crumpled, just like she'd rolled out of bed, which she had I guess. But now she'd done her hair and make-up and wow, she looked neat. I swear, I had to lean forward so no one could see how the crotch of my dirty jeans was pointing right up off the seat.

So Pretty Chick took my mind right off ol' Thin Lips, and I watched her for the rest of the meeting. She had this soft little neck, the kind you'd have fun running your jaw along, you know when you haven't shaved for a few days, and it's not proper beard yet, but it's all soft and stubbly. And the chick giggles and says you tickle, but doesn't pull away. And yeah then I won't deny it, I was thinking of how it would be if we were both standing pitch naked in one of the camp showers - not that there are many of them, you're supposed to make do with a bowl of water and go home every now and again for a proper wash – but just supposing it was late at night and there wasn't a queue, and we just snuck in, and she soaped me down, and of course it being all in my head she doesn't gag at the scent of the dirty toilets I've still got on my scrubbing hands, and we get all soapy and wet, and then – because it is a dream -

"What do you think, Hape?" And oh shit, the meeting leader's asking me a question. I open my eyes. Hell, I hope I was only dribbling in my dream. Look down at my jeans. Could be worse, at least they're still dry.

"I dunno, I mean, I'm in favour of whatever the majority want," I say hastily.

Everyone laughs, as if I've said something funny. I can't be doing with looking a fool, so I ditch the stupid meeting, head down towards the road towards the end of the camp. There's a Māori Warden, and she calls out "all right, love?" I nod curtly. Next I pass a fancy woman wrapped up in a blanket that has stars and unicorns on it, looks like she's just dropped in out of Fairyland.

"Hi!" she says brightly as I pass. "Would you like me to tell you a story?"

I shake my head, trying not to open my mouth in case I say something rude. I walk a bit further, past some student artist who's decided her urgent and essential contribution to the cause is to stick gaudy protest collages all over the dry-stone wall. Someone ought to dob her in for cultural vandalism. The last group is a bunch of guys in leathers. They're leaning against motorbikes, we all know who they belong to, but if the Mob wanna turn up and support the protest, who's going to tell them to go away?

Then it's empty land, I'm walking down towards the village, and as soon as I decently can, I hop the fence and head into the fields. There's a river, well it's not a river any more, just a polluted bit of grime, plastics factory pissing its waste into the river. But it's got a bank, out of sight, and then I'm lying down, biting my hands and arms, ripping at my flesh with all the fury and pain I don't want to forget, marking my body to make sure, damn sure, I remember the pain, because no one is going to tell me bygones are bygones, not whilst that bastard is still alive.

And then after a few minutes I'm conscious that it's sore,

and I've done enough damage for now, and I'm not gonna lie, I was in tears. Snot and blood and sweat and the stains of toilet shit. I'm telling you, I was in a right mess.

Someone has come up close without my hearing. I realise they're there, because the sun's suddenly blotted out. I'm scared it's old Maggot, but when I turn round there are a nice pair of rounded lips, surrounded by a moko that covers his pleasant face. Now of course I'm relieved, but at the same time, you know? Some bros moko their whole face because they're spiritual and holy and love the whenua and tradition. And others do it because they're with the gangs. I didn't know which group this guy was, so I was ants in my pants for what he wanted with me, and why he'd followed me all the way out here.

But he didn't say anything. Just sat down, took a ciggie out of his leather jacket pocket and offered me one. We sat and smoked together.

After a bit he pointed to my arms. "You don't wanna do that to yourself, bro. They're beating us up enough already."

I shook my head. "Gotta make sure I don't forget. Making a promise I can't walk away from. That's what it is."

I didn't say anything more, and he didn't ask. He just took me off to the First Aid stop where my cuts were treated by this bonkers old nurse who's taken her crappy broken-down caravan to every single protest they've had in New Zealand for the last fifty years. She asked us what had happened and he said I'd fallen into some brambles. There's no brambles around here but she knew enough not to ask again.

When they were all dressed she asked me if I was cold. Stupid question, we were all freezing. So she took me out the back to this tent where they were giving out hot water bottles. With covers knitted by old ladies from the community centre, specially for the protest. And we waited for the water to boil, in this dodgy old boiler that looked like it might explode. But you're not going to believe it, it was a taonga. They'd brought it down from Bastion Point. It had done hot water bottles for those old bros too.

It was all so good and heartfelt and wanting to make the world a better place. It wasn't like that daft bitch with her silly fairytales, or the police standing there with stones instead of faces. It was us, all of us, coming together. Going for what was right, not for what was easy. Doing the mahi, hoping we'd get the treats.

But I wasn't in the mood. I didn't want to be a protector. Not at any cost. It's nice to play by the rules, but you can't trust whitey to do the same. Look at what happened at Parihaka. And besides…

I wanted utu, man.

River Time
Late Phanerozoic
(The Eon of Visible Life)

There are the people of the water, the land, the fire and the air. There are those who drift in currents to and from the places they inhabit. They follow books, churches, quarrelling pastors, angry rabbis. They hear of a better imam or a wiser tohunga and they take sail to a separate sea. These are not the peoples of the book, although the wiser ones among them know that letters are but a sea of faith, and no one but the dead or insane truly can claim knowledge of whatever land lies on the other side.

There are the people who ride boats or fly kites with a rush of joy in the today. They swoop down mountains and breathe strange gases in the depths of the sea. They hear of a new land of adventure, and immediately they need to travel. These are not the peoples of the waves, although the wiser ones know how much time and energy the wave-finders took to walk their ships with star-maps across an earlier sea.

There are the people who set urupa in caves and hollows with a knowing and belonging. They touch the kumara and the potato with fiery care. Where they walk, the ground grows fertile and fallow below their digging sticks. These are not the peoples of the land, although the whenua knows them as its own. They are wiser than the rest because they know nothing at all, other than what they do not know: they are of dust, and to dust they shall return.

Last of all come the fire-gatherers, the spirit-bringers, the people of the fiery lakes. They walk with the dead and the unborn, the unholy darkness that burns in the heart of the silent city, the trembling ache that rises with a taniwha's lava foam from inland lakes of lava and red-hot snow. They sleep where Papatuānuku's crust is thinnest, and their dreams curl upwards with the choking smoke of the underworld below.

Ihumātao called them all, as if it was a home and a forgetting. They came in dribbles, drops of water. They fell onto the waiting land like spray crashing out of the sea. You could say these were different parts of Aotearoa, or different plants in the sea. Or you could say they were different stories, from the same person, the same reason for protesting, expressed in a dozen ways. All of these, and none of them, would be true. There was room for all of them, just as there is always room for me, the endless river, to rush into the waiting sea

2019
Te Kotahitanga Marae,
West Waikato

Only two days in, and already the floor of the campervan was so covered with shards of potato chips and sand that you could scarcely see the floor. Ugh, thought Adele, stepping gingerly over a pair of Mark's dirty socks. I know I don't keep my room tidy at home, but it's less gross when you're just wading through your own mess.

"Come on, seatbelts on, off we go," exclaimed Sheila. "What's the schedule say today, Ben?"

"Oh, I've got thrilling news," he deadpanned, looking up from the computer printout. "Apparently, our next stop is Meremere. Just like Paris, except without all the interesting bits."

Rosemary shook a warning fist at him from the back seat.

"Well, not quite," he continued, grinning. "There may not be the Louvre or la Tour Eiffel, but Meremere was the site of the first coal-fired power station in New Zealand."

Mark sagged in his seat. "Can we go home?"

Ignoring them, Sheila switched on the ignition. It was a second hand import vehicle, that yelped apologetically in Japanese every time they turned it on. "All right, let's get going. Anyone who complains gets assigned to portaloo cleaning duties."

Adele, Ben and Mark slouched mutinously in their seats.

After an abortive attempt to suggest that they all played *I Spy* or *Red Car Yellow Car*, the mothers seemed to work out that the driving part of this road trip would be better if they left their offspring to doze and text in peace. There was an almost companionable silence for an hour, as they trundled slowly along the Waikato banks.

"So peaceful," exclaimed Rosemary.

When grownups say somewhere is peaceful, thought Adele irritably, what they mean is dull. No wonder New Zealand has no history. Cows and power stations, that's all that ever happened here. I bet being born in the past was even duller than now. She closed her eyes.

"Oh, here we are." Sheila swung over.

Rosemary looked alarmed. "What are you doing?"

"Te Kotahitanga Marae. Saw it on the map. I thought we'd stop and have a look."

"Why?" Rosemary's voice was cold.

Adele opened her eyes and glanced out. *Oh. A rural marae.*

"You'll like this, Adele. Won't you." Cynthia spoke hopefully.

"Yeah." Adele scowled. "I feel really at home and in touch with my cultural heritage already. Would you like me to do a haka too?"

Cynthia gave her a look, and she clambered out of the van. Rosemary followed her looking worriedly at the carvings on the wall. She touched Ben's shoulder, and her lips moved in what Adele guessed was a protective prayer. Only Mark and Sheila seemed at all pleased that they had stopped.

Mark grinned happily. "Look at that cool sculpture. I want to have one like that at home."

Jutting up from the roof, a carved red figure pointed a spear at the clear blue sky. Anger or protection?

"Do you know what it means, Adele?" Sheila asked politely.

Adele gave an exclamation of impatience. "I haven't

seen my dad since I was five. How the hell would I know?"

"Let's get moving, shall we? Not much to see here." Rosemary was evidently off on one of her devil-worship benders. If they didn't drive on soon she'd probably feel compelled to exorcise the campervan.

"No." Sheila looked at her firmly. "I want to show Mark the inside."

The ground was slushy and damp. Adele wondered if it was wetlands or flooding. Probably not rain, there hadn't been any for a while. Maybe freshwater wetlands. She wondered what fish lived here, and how the locals had managed to build a marae on such soggy ground. "Photo us outside it. Go on." Mark was grinning as if he had caught a fish.

Rosemary shook her head. "I'm afraid we can't take photos here, Mark. Some iwis have the tradition that photography is disrespectful in a tapu place and look, there's a sign up here saying so."

Adele wished she had known that. It was her heritage, after all. That was the problem with being bicultural, like New Zealand: you got all the problems of both cultures but you never had the time to learn enough to understand both well. Perhaps bicultural was now an outdated idea. There were Chinese, and Koreans, and Indians. Maybe they would start building their temples, if they hadn't already. A billion more places for her to feel that she didn't belong. And she would wander around the outsides of more religious structures, never going in to do more than take a photograph, or not even that if they were funny about it. Still, at least no one would ask her to explain the meaning of a mosque, or say a Hindu prayer like that awful time the arts group leader had asked her to open home school group with a karakia.

The marae looked blank and empty. Red carvings pointed at the sky. Like a jigsaw, only standing outside it was as if some of the pieces were missing.

"The gate's closed, I'm afraid."

Mark began to climb over the fence.

"Don't." Rosemary was obviously afraid the heathen devils that lived in the marae would come out and spirit him off.

"She's right, Mark, it's not respectful." Sheila tugged at his pants. "You wouldn't like it if someone came and broke into shul."

"They do," Mark reminded her. "Remember the night the mad guy with a knife who wanted to kill the Jews came? And we sat and sang stupid songs for ages with the doors locked till the police came?"

"Yes, exactly." Sheila shuddered. "So you should know how it feels."

"Oh, ridiculous." Scorn suddenly surged through Rosemary's bright veneer. "They get more than enough respect these days. Scholarships and special schools in their own language and their own departments in hospitals – they want the airwaves and always trying to get the water to make money, they even argued about the beach – and it's not enough for them to have their own TV channel, now we have to hear them squawking in their own dialect on our news as well –"

There was a ghastly silence. She tailed off. Everyone looked at Adele, and then tried to pretend they weren't. Rosemary's eyes flickered slightly, as she realised who was present. Then she gave an attempt at a brave, inclusive smile.

"That is, Adele. Obviously I don't mean you."

Adele wanted to smile and say forget it. But she also wanted to clout Rosemary, and then perhaps be sick.

This was, as she and Cynthia often bemoaned together, one of the problems with the home education community. It was very, very, white. And it was also very insular. If you believed that global warming wasn't real or that Māori were inferior to Pākehā, the chances were you did not meet many people who could challenge you. Except bloody me, Adele. Who doesn't fit in with the white world and knows nothing about anything else. Perhaps I don't belong with Cynthia at all, she thought bitterly. Perhaps I should go and live somewhere else.

It was the kind of thought that gave her bad dreams later. As if she'd willed what happened next.

"All right," said Sheila after a pause, "let's get moving. We want to be at Meremere by sunset. I understand there was quite a battle there," she commented.

"Yes," Ben interjected eagerly, "there's some papers about it in the box. Look let's have a quick look."

He reached into the back of the campervan storage area, and brought out a white box. As he opened it, Rosemary gave a loud wail.

"Oh Ben, not the skull-cracker. I told you to leave that abominable monstrosity at home."

The taiaha glistened invitingly. It was beautiful, amber-studded and polished smooth by generations of hands. Afterwards, Ben wondered why it had been placed at the very top of the box. Almost as if it wanted to be found. Adele stared. She didn't think she'd ever seen such a beautiful taonga before. It was even better than the ones in the Auckland museum.

Mark reached forward and seized the polished blade. He swirled it around his head. "Watch me, I'm a warrior, I'm gonna kill you all!" he screamed.

Rosemary grabbed it from him. She screamed as she did so, as if it burnt her hands. And with a vicious flourish, flung it in the direction of the river.

It didn't quite go the full distance. Instead, it landed with a loud crash on the ground.

Ben ran and picked it up.

"You put that down!" yelled Rosemary. Spittle whirred from her lips.

Ben held the taiaha in his hands, uncertainly.

"I can see devils! Devils are all around you! Son, you're possessed!" Rosemary threw her arms into the air. "Maranatha, Lord Jesus, come and rid this cursed tribe, as you cleansed Israel of sin cleanse us now!" she gibbered. "Horns and teeth. I can see them, all around us, rubbing their hands with glee."

Sheila stepped forward and put a reassuring hand on her arm. "It's all right, Rosemary. Just take a couple of deep breaths. We're all safe. No devils here."

Rosemary whirled around, dribbling with rage. "Woe upon you, Scribes, Rabbis and Pharisees! Repent! Understand and accept the Lord Jesus Christ! All of you, all of you are damned, do you not understand! And now you've taken my son!"

There was another awful pause, broken, of course, by Mark. "So, like, it's interesting with the Pharisees, they were just the scholars who knew a lot about Torah." He giggled. "Do you know, they talk about pubes in the Talmud."

Sheila shook her head at him, and for once, he seemed to realise that he needed to be quiet.

Rosemary turned back to Ben. "I said, repent. Jesus came to lay a sword between father and son. I won't have an infidel in my home. Put it down."

Ben hesitated. Then shook his head. "No. Not if you're going to throw it away."

"I'll take it." Cynthia marched forward. Gratefully, Ben gave her the taiaha. A couple of amber kauri gum pearls dropped from it. Cynthia scrambled to pick them up from the ground.

He slouched towards the campervan, not meeting his mother's eye. As he approached, Adela saw that in the scramble, a shirtsleeve had slipped up. The marks were still there, but they were fading. Adele waited for someone else to comment, but they were obviously all gripped by the unfolding psychological drama in front of them.

There was a long pause, whilst everyone waited to see

what Rosemary would do next. She didn't seem completely sure either. Eventually she punched the air with a faint "Hallelujah!" and then immediately burst into tears.

"Well." Sheila broke the awkward silence. "Looks like we've discovered a national treasure. I suppose the best thing to do is to drop that off at the next museum we come to. Is there one in Meremere, Cynthia?"

Cynthia nodded. "Also, I, uh, I was interested in what Mark was saying in the car about the old storekeeper at Port Waikato." Sheila talked hastily as they unpacked the parental bags from the cars, as if history could cover the embarrassment of the present. "He had a Jewish name, Curren. If his family has been in the business a while it's likely he is descended from some of the earliest Port Jew traders. Do you know what that is, Adele?"

"I want a photo." Mark was in one of his stuck record moods. Sheila raised her phone.

"A proper one. Not by you."

"All right, Adele can take one of you against the river. Not the marae. OK?"

Adele started to look for her camera, trying to zone out Sheila's nervous educational drone.

"Well, in the nineteenth century Jews were still very discriminated against in England. So some Jews were among the earliest settlers. Many set up trading stores in remote areas where they could sell to both the local tribes and passing ships. That is why they were called Port Jews."

Yeah, whatever. Her camera was still in the van. She'd have to step over all those crunchy potato chips again. Cursing, she climbed back in to pick it up. As she did so, something flickered in the distance and drew her eye. Not something. Someone: a white ute, at the back of the marae. And in it, a man. Almost not there, nearly out of sight, half hidden behind the trees. Just like the man in the photograph, at the bottom of the cliffs, who might just possibly have been a smudge. Looking at him, Adele felt her neck prickle, the same weird sensation that she had whenever her social worker or lawyer came to ask her questions about home schooling. It was as if she was in danger, but she was not quite sure why.

She would like to have decided that, like the smudge and Rosemary's devils, the whole business was in her imagination. But this time he was not in a photograph, but sitting in a truck. Just behind them, on the other side of the road. Thin lips, and maggoty white skin. A computer out, pretending to do some work, but really he was watching them all steadily. And Adele was quite sure that he was real.

1862

Meremere

Bellbirds kittered in the tree canopy above their heads. Late afternoon, and at last there was something new to see beyond the endless river and forest. It was a great green hill, looming above them. It looked ugly and half-artificial, not surprising, Thomas learnt later, because it was already the site of a semi-fortified pa. Across the Waikato, such fortifications were being built to provide a line of defence, if the British marched south.

"All right, boys. Get out here."

Mr James sounded tired and irritable. That wasn't surprising. The journey had been exhausting. The boat had arrived at dawn. Matua had asked one of the Māori oarsmen if he would carry a message to his father back at Port Waikato, but the oarsman was a crony of Mr James and had translated the request for the schoolmaster's benefit. Matua received several kicks in the stomach from them both that made Thomas' own stomach hurt. He spat up a little bit of blood.

"Feeling better now?" asked Mr James. "You look like a gutted fish." And he launched into a long ramble about how one place he'd been, the locals used to prope up a man so they could watch their insides being dragged out. They'd leave him to die with his guts all wrapped around a tree, just like bloody lengths of rope. Matua glared, but did not speak.

After a long day of watching the Waikato slap pointlessly

at the sides of the boat, they had arrived at their destination
A small white-washed hotel and trading post.

"Where are we?" Thomas asked.

"Meremere, rotten little place, filled with defiant natives.
Hopefully soon Cameron and Grey will come down and
get them under control. Can you believe, they've only been
and brought up cannon from Raglan. Our cannon. Taken
from our ships. Cheeky bastards. They think they can hold
us back with a bit of gunpowder and earth."

"I believe that reports from the North suggest that
actually some of my people have been quite effective at
holding the Empire back with a bit of gunpowder and earth.
For quite a long time," Matua muttered to Thomas under
his breath. "And what about Taranaki? We've had them on
the run for a couple of years."

Thomas nodded. He hoped that Matua would see sense
and shut up. Valour is all very well in the heat of battle, but
unless Matua had a cunning plan to stop Mr James hitting
him on the head again, this conversational direction did
not seem a good idea. But to his relief, for once the stick
did not crack anywhere near either of them. Perhaps Mr
James was too tired to be riled about politics.Or perhaps he
simply hadn't heard.

"Just get out, the pair of you. Matua, carry my bags into
the hotel. Ask for my room and wait for me there. Thomas,
you stay with me whilst I see to the horses. Matua, I know
your people are fond of running away from the battlefield
but do try to take your punishment like a man and stay with
us tonight. If you make a run for it I assure you that I will
break both of Thomas's legs."

Thomas watched Matua's straight back disappear into
the hotel. His head was throbbing now, like rushing water.

"Where are we going to stay tonight, Sir?"

"Matua is going to sleep in the stables with the horses
and the dogs. Where he belongs. He'll be locked in so he
won't escape." He looked down at Thomas with that strange

sudden appearance of fondness. "Don't worry. I'm not treating you like a native. You are going to share a room with me."

Thomas was too tired and dizzy to decide whether this was a good or a bad thing, but Mr James was holding him quite firmly by the arm so he didn't think he had much choice. They walked around to the back of the hotel, where some shillings changed hands and the stable hand promised to give Matua some horseshit to shovel and to beat him like a blackamoor if he tried to get away.

There was good news for Mr James' pocket, too, the stable hand told them. The boat they had used to get here would be easily returned. By good fortune another visitor from Port Waikato was staying at the hotel tonight, a Jewish trader travelling down river. He would be delighted to hire the boat on his return. Mr James looked oddly worried at this news, but did not demur.

The hotel was dark, and oakpanelled, like the taverns Thomas remembered from Ireland. Men left their boots at the door. Socks were rarely changed, so the place stank to high heaven, whatever that was like. Matua was waiting inside. He looked strangely cowed.

"Ah, boy." Mr James was suddenly affable again. "I presume they have shown you to my room to put my bags away." Matua nodded.

"It's done, sir."

"And why are you not waiting there for me? As I told you?"

Matua looked past him, as if trying to catch a glimpse of the free hills outside.

"They said I couldn't, sir. No natives allowed inside the hotel."

Here in the Pākehā world, Thomas realised, Matua was vulnerable in a way he, Thomas, was not. No one knew his father was a great chief who parried the jealous thrusts of Pākehā and rival authorities with brilliant strategic skill. No one would suspect that his people owned fertile land and were such skilled farmers that his hapu sold tonnes of fruit and vegetables every year to Auckland. Here, he was just a native. He could be twenty or thirty years old, and the settlers would still speak to him as "boy."

"Good, good." Mr James patted him on the head. "Now, bearing in mind the important political point you made a few minutes ago, I have made a special arrangement with the stable hands. They have found quite a bit of earth for you to play in. Horseshit, to be precise. Afraid there's no gunpowder, but we'll have to make do. You can practice your warrior trenchdigging skills by cleaning out the stables for a few hours. Then you can sleep in it tonight." He chuckled benignly, as if at a shared joke.

It would get better, Thomas thought desperately. Mr James was terrible, but surely the school itself would not be so bad. He would not be the only teacher. Māori boarding schools had a good reputation. They were not prisons, but prestigious places. Run by missionaries, they were welcomed by the Māori in areas of high European settlement as a way to ensure their children learnt English. Matua's father had once discussed with Father Murphy whether his iwi might possibly donate land for such a school, on the condition that traditional values were respected and conversion to Christiantiy was not a prerequisite for attendance. But that was before all the trouble started.

The heat of the fire was warming his body, and, he suspected, befuddling his thinking. Now he was inside and warm, sleep and boarding school tomorrow did not seem so bad. Mr James had been awful this morning, but over the course of the day, things had improved. For Thomas, at least. Now it was evening, and he was almost friendly. Perhaps it was only Māori he hated. Odd, then, that he wanted to teach in a Māori school. Perhaps that was why he was taking Thomas, so he would have some Pākehā company. He was stroking Thomas' head again, and saying something about him having the same beautiful shade of hair as his sister. The landlord was giving them both strange looks.

It was funny, because although he had visited and courted her all last winter, Thomas had had the feeling that he wasn't quite as much in love with Mary as he said. Father had even said, he's a funny fish Mary, an established professional man and all that, but be careful. I'm not sure how much warmth you'll get from him longterm. Now he knew Father must have been wrong. He must have been very much in love because he seemed to be fond of Thomas just because he looked like his sister. He probably had a deep passion and now he had a broken heart. Thomas almost felt sorry for him but then he remembered Matua outside digging in the yard.

If only his head didn't ache so much. He was very tired. Mr James took him to the corner of the bar, where there was a stool. He sat him down. Now he was being kind again, and even buying him a drink. It was all very confusing. Mr James didn't drink, Thomas knew that, but here he was offering Thomas a nice beer, to take away the headache and make him sleep well. Thomas didn't want the beer but he also didn't want to be outside digging horseshit like Matua. Better just to let Mr James be kind. Things might be easier.

He finished the beer, and realised he had drunk on an empty stomach, which was something his father said you should never do. Now he was very tired. Mr James was taking him by the hand again, and leading him upstairs, very kindly, and making soft murmuring noises about soon he would be asleep. Maybe he had made a mistake, and he was a good man after all. A stout woman in a bonnet passed them. "Is everything all right?"

"My son, he's unwell," he heard Mr James say. "Got hit on the head today."

"Poor little mite. Make sure he rests."

"I will do. Keep him with me tonight."

He stumbled up the last few stairs. At the top, Mr James

fumbled in his pocket for the key. He was trembling, Thomas noticed. As if afraid. No, not afraid. Almost excited. Like when one of the boat lads looked at Thomas' sister. Inside, the bedroom was small. A wash jug stood in the corner.

"Get undressed and wash yourself," said Mr James. He shoved Thomas towards the corner of the room.

Thomas was used to swimming naked in the river, and of course he and his siblings shared baths at home. But this didn't feel like that. He dawdled, trying to unlace his boots as slowly as possible. Maybe Mr James would get bored soon and go away.

"Hurry up."

Reluctantly, Thomas took off his shirt, then his breeches. He didn't wear anything underneath.

"Good. Now wash yourself. No skimping. I don't want to be paying extra for dirty sheets." He placed his hands on Thomas' bare shoulders. They were, Thomas noticed, shaking. "No, that's not clean enough. Start again."

Thomas tried to clean his bits and pieces thoroughly, but it was difficult with someone watching him. "Not like that." Mr James sounded patient and kind. Here. Give me the soap. I'll show you what to do." Mr James was just reaching out with trembling hands towards the part of Thomas' body that Matua called the ure when there was an insistent knock on the door.

"What now?" he shouted impatiently in the general direction of the staircase.

"I'm sorry sir." Matua's voice, shaking and subservient. "The trader – from Port Waikato – Cohen he needs to speak to you urgently about the boat."

Mr James made an exclamation of disgust. "That old Port Jew? Can't he wait until morning?"

"No, sir. I said you were very tired. He said it couldn't wait, he wants to leave tonight and he needs to see you beforehand. I tried to deal with it myself but he said he said he needed you."

"Oh, for goodness sake." Mr James flung a cold hand around Thomas' shoulder. "These stingy Jews. Stay undressed and get into bed. I'll wash you properly when I get back."

Thomas did as he was told. His head was now spinning so much he couldn't see the ceiling properly. He doubted he would be conscious for long.

Then Matua's voice, urgently, rousing him. "Get up, Thomas. You're naked, get dressed. You have to escape, right now. Thank the gods that Cohen was passing by. I told him what James was up to with you tonight, no surprise apparently, he's known for it.

"Cohen's going to keep him talking in the bar. Try to get him drunk if possible so he doesn't notice you're gone. The stable hands are going to swear that I was there with them all the time. I told them you were Irishborn and that he was after your backside. They'll get you down to the river. Get a boat home. Tell everybody what Mr James tried to do."

"But – but." Thomas tried to collect his thoughts. "You're the one who should run away. He's making you shovel shit. He's being nice to me."

Matua dragged him out of bed. "No he isn't. I can't run away or he'll have my father arrested. But you must."

"He bought me beer even though he doesn't drink. He said he would educate me properly."

"No. This is much worse than anything he's going to do to me."

"I don't understand."

"Oh sweet Rongomatane, now is not the time. We have to get going."

Thomas shook his head. "Not without you. Not unless you explain."

"Look, men love men as well as women. Or instead of. You get that? That has always happened. It's normal." Matua sucked his teeth. "If you want the truth, that's one of the reasons my father doesn't want our family to convert, because your tohunga forbid it. And he lay with men when he was young, and he knows we may want to do the same."

Thomas struggled to keep his eyes open. He tried to speak but his tongue was slow. "What? You mean me and you - "

Matua interrupted. "Me, all right? He knows that's what I want. You know I've been a bastard to you these last few months. The thing is, I was starting to feel that way for you myself, and -"

"Me?"

"Yes, you. I'm sorry. I didn't want you to know. But can't you see, I was trying to make sure you didn't feel the same way about me. Not yet. Because you're young, and maybe that's not what you want, and it's trouble with your tohunga if we're found, and I wanted to leave you free to decide on your own."

Thomas remembered the time Matua had stroked his ear, the soft gentleness, and the sudden jerking away.

"So that's why I beat you up so much, all right? To stop you wanting me before you were ready. But Mr James wants the opposite. He'll take you before you can decide, and that's not fine. Not here, not in your country, not in Rome or Hawaiiki. It will tear you, it will break you, it will damage you for a lifetime. In tinana and wairua, body and spirit." He spat. "Put your clothes on. Now."

River Time,
At Various Geological Seasons

I, the Waikato, run through many lands. Not just your land, today's economy, buildings and dotted cowfields: but older, deeper ones, the lands that crack down into the depths of the riverbed, below the silt, and the debris, and the lost skulls of forgotten wars. My currents sift the waves between surface and the deep, past and present.

Most of you only travel in one time. That is your destiny. You see revenge as one who must accomplish the blood debt in your lifetime. You see whānau as those who are alive around you.

But that is not the only way to ride the rivers, and not the only way to travel the darkness time. Sometimes when Kupe slew the waters with his canoe, he saw strange figures on the opposite banks. This land was not yet inhabited by the human race, and yet he could see metallic sparks as a great iron road was hammered painstakingly into the soil.

Other times the Great Journey was punctuated with screams of one people attacking another. Up north there lies a cave, where all is lost and dark. So it should be, because it is where a woman was betrayed. A woman who ran away from her cruel husband and took shelter with another people who dwelt in the hills. A violent man who wanted his unwilling wife back, and was prepared to fight to the death in order to have her. The chief of the hill people was herself a woman, but she surrendered the refugee rather than sacrifice her people. There is only so much generosity in the human heart, only so much space in your homes for the outsider.

I am the running river, yes, but I am also the ancestor of all the children who run wild through the houses and streets of this concrete tangata tiriti land, seeking a home to feel free. That is how Hape felt, as he lay on the turtle's back. The turtle came and picked him up, whilst he wept in grief at his abandonment on the shores of Hawaiiki. Yes, he whispered as they set off in the dismal solitude of the ocean, without family or friends. I will let this turtle whāngai me. I will find a home where I can be free.

2019

Hamilton

"I'm so sorry about what Rosemary said earlier today, Adele." Cynthia took her outside for a quiet chat as soon as they reached the motel. Garish neon lights promised that there was a vacancy. It turned her head an awkward red shade. Like a very apologetic prostitute, Adele thought.

"It's fine." That's what you say when your mum messes up. Even if it sort of isn't.

"We'll go home tomorrow, all right? Get Sheila to drive us to Hamilton and catch a bus home. I should probably stop pissing off my lawyer anyway."

"All right."

"Unless you want to stay."

Adele thought about it. The feelings inside her weren't going to get better by leaving. They splashed around anyway, cold and snaky. And then, there was Ben. "Look, the thing is. I'm worried about Ben."

"So are we all."

"No, not about today. I mean his mental health."

"Well yes. Living with that woman, no other influences, locked up twenty four seven –"

"Look, the thing is - "

Then she saw him, crumpled up helplessly against the wall.

"Jesus." Cynthia ran forward. "Are you ok?"

Adele knelt down next to him. "Hey, what's up, ballbreaker?"

He was pale and didn't meet her eyes. The motel ferns whispered behind her in the wind.

"I can't," he whispered. "I just can't do it any more."

"Do what?"

"All of it."

"Mate, if you don't like the road trip any more, bale. We're leaving anyway. You can chill with us for a few days if you need. Go home when things have calmed down."

He shook his head vigorously. "All of it." His speech was slightly slurred.

A horrible cold suspicion began to settle in her mind. "Ben, what have you taken?"

"Nothing."

"I mean it, Ben, what have you taken? Tell me the truth, or I'm calling an ambulance."

He slurred again. "Not taken anything. Not yet. These things – just keep happening –"

For a moment, the wild thought occurred to her that perhaps Rosemary was right, and that a demon had settled in Ben's head.

But Cynthia was calm and practical. "Ben, you're ill. I'm calling your mum."

"No. I'm fine."

"You are so not fine."

"Leave me alone. You're a bitch."

Adele blinked in astonishment. It could not have been more out of character if he'd drawn a knife and threatened to stab her.

Cynthia crouched down next to him, and spoke very slowly, as if to a small child. "OK, you hold Adele's hand and stay here, OK? I'm going to speak to your mum now. Try to relax. We have to get you to hospital."

He shrugged slightly, as if not caring too much where he went, and huddled down again against the brick wall.

2019

Mangere Bridge

It took me the rest of the morning to find Pretty Chick again. Eventually I spotted her, back in the lunch tent. Man, that girl really liked her coffee. It wasn't too hard to sidle up next to her and ask her how she was sleeping at night, and what did she think about the mint fresh cappuccino van that was doling out free coffee to protestors.

She thought it was a good thing, no surprise there, but mainly she was worried because she didn't have any spare clothes. Turned out she and her mate had come down from the Far North on a whim. They'd been listening to the news on telly whilst they were outside having a cig, late at night, then one of them said, yeah we should be down there, and the other one, she agreed. So like a pair of bosses – and I mean that in the good way – they got into their old banger and drove through the night. Got here at seven a.m., just in time for breakfast. No wonder she was keen on the free coffee.

I offered to show her around, and she said she'd love to in a bit, but first she had to go back to her mate's car and send some texts, let her parents know where she was, that kind of thing. All well and good. She walks off and I'm just realising I haven't nailed the deal. We didn't set a time or place to meet, but what do you know the old geezer who runs the kitchen comes up and asks if I mind shifting some crates of fresh food that've just come in.

So I do my bit, and then follow in the direction she's

gone. Doesn't take long to spot her big Far North farm gumboots outside one of the cars on the verge. I saunter up, getting ready to pretend I've just like passed by on my way to the village for a sandwich. But the curtains are shut and inside there's this groaning moaning sound, *yeah babe, give it to me*, like that, yeah. Just like in my daydream but with the crucial difference that no one's invited me to get involved.

Shit I feel a fool. Especially when I – yeah, don't judge me, I haven't had a chick since I came home to live with Mum and Sis, I was desperate, get me, I only wanted to listen, see, it's not like I was planning to be a peeping Tom – so it's these curtains, right, they're a DIY job, not properly attached, and what with the ruckus inside someone's bare arse comes up against the window and knocks one of them down. You couldn't not see, if you were standing right beside it. Which I was.

Anyway it was two girls. Her and her mate. Ha. Nice line that she fed me. Her and her girlie fuck-buddy, more like. They were both naked and sweaty and into it. I don't know if they saw me but I was out of there as fast as my legs could carry me. Turned my stomach a bit. I mean I know it happens but I'd never seen it like that up close. Some men like watching them at it but not me. I don't see why they've got to go at it like that. It's not like there's not plenty of men in the world.

I'd been kinda fantasising about hanging around and beating the shit out of whatever guy she was nailing. But that wasn't going to happen now. So I walked off. And instead I started thinking about what I was gonna to do to Thin-Lips, if and when I managed to get hold of him.

Hold him down, that would be the first thing. Stare into his petrified pebbly eyes, just the way he used to do to me. Then I'd hold a razor to his face, and just when he started to whimper with fear, then slowly, very slowly, I'd cut off his eyebrows. Shave him, slowly, making sure to make a few nicks, and then I'd make him strip down and shave off every damn pube on his horrible wrinkled little scrotum. He'll be crying then, begging me to stop. But I won't stop, not until I've shaved off a fair bit of skin too. And then I'm going to get out my big butcher's knife, and slowly, ever so slowly, slit open his guts. Just like he was a piece of fish.

I suggest you skip this paragraph if you have a delicate mind. Because when you gut a fish, you do it quickly. But I'd spend hours on it. I wouldn't just gut him open so he bled and lost consciousness. Oh no, I'd beat him up a little bit first. I'd make him all bruised and bloody on the inside and out. Then I'd stamp on him, hands and feet, and when all those little delicate bones were broken I'd start breaking the bigger ones too. He'd still be conscious, but if I was doing a good job he wouldn't be making much sense. His teeth I'd leave in until the end. Because it's weird, if you pull out a tooth it doesn't matter if a person's near dead, they'll still wake up and start screaming. It's the worst torture you've got, so you leave it until last. After that you split the stomach, gently. And if you've timed it right, the tooth pain has roused him good and proper. So you can prop him up and let him watch you pull his own guts into gory tomato-coloured spaghetti shapes on the ground.

All right, delicate ones, you can start reading again now. Just as long as you remember, that every single thing I've got planned for Thin-Lips is a butterfly's piss in the ocean compared to what he did to me.

2019

Hamilton

Soon, the ambulance shrieks. Affable St John's staff dismount, breathless and windswept. As if they'd ridden through the bush on postilion horses, rather than driving through a suburb of South Hamilton. Rosemary babbles nonsense at them, and they quickly ascertain that Adele and Cynthia are the ones who've kept their cool. A vision of podgy-cheeked diligence, they check Ben's pupils and reflexes. "He seems confused. Did he take something? Or hit his head?"

Adele shakes her head. "I didn't see it if he did. And we've been together all afternoon."

Rosemary makes the obligatory telephone call home to her husband, and rides with Adele and Ben in the ambulance. Everyone else follows in the campervan. Adele doesn't really want to hang out with Rosemary the Racist. But she ends up agreeing to get in the ambulance too, because Ben is babbling like a child now, and won't let go of her hand.

River Time
Post-Pleistocene

Now the river is roaring, and for the first time in all his travels, Kupe is afraid. He has seen the Waikato as a gift from the land, but now it is as if he has voyaged too far, too deeply, and the waters have taken umbrage and threatened to cover him up. "I will name you, wild country," he yells at the waters. "I will discover you for my people and name each of your rocks and valleys, one by one. You will not defeat me with your wiles." But the river roars, and his head hurts with the noise, and he is afraid.

Kupe was not as strong as he looked. But Hape, he was the opposite. To his family and people he was weak, a liability. That is why they left him asleep, blocking up the windows and running away to sea. But Hape was stronger than all of them, because he had rage. Rage it was that drew the turtle to him, and rage it was that kept them both afloat on the impossible wandering vastness of the sea. Rage is not always what you expect. It lies underfoot, the heated earth of the thin-crust islands, the flushing skin of the kid who doesn't dare to answer back. The silent one, the forgotten one, the story that has never been told, the boy with the clubfoot. The turtle rider, the dream-wayfarer. The man who arrived first after all, took the fertile lands of Ihumātao for himself.

And did he forgive his people, and let them settle with him, on this fertile blessed piece of land? Did he hell. They arrived in a cringing apologetic mass. Expecting to be forgiven. But he would have none of it. He stood up on his club foot, and roared like an angry bull and drove them out. Was he right or wrong? Should whānau always forgive? The story is silent on that point, like a secret that must never be told.

1862

Meremere

"I'm not going without you." Thomas was sure of that. "If he's bad like you say, he means harm to us both."

Matua swore at him in Māori, and pulled him out of bed.

"I don't care," Thomas said, standing naked in the middle of the room.

Matua looked pointedly out of the window. Afterwards, when he remembered, he found the scene quite comical. At the time he was just embarrassed that his uru was so small in the evening cold. "I'm not putting a stitch on until you agree to come too."

"I can't, don't you see? My father. I couldn't' bear them sending him to jail."

"If they're going to do it, they'll do it anyway. Whether Mr James makes you his slave or not."

Matua considered the point, and spread his arms in reluctant acquiescence. "All right. We'll go together. But only because you are such a naïve goat you wouldn't have a hope of getting far on your own. Now will you get your clothes on before he comes upstairs to have another go?"

They tiptoed down the corridor and down the staircase. They were just about to go outside, when Matua pushed Thomas sharply behind an armoire, of the grand carved wooden kind that had sat squatly in the deep hull of the ship that had brought them out from Ireland. They squashed together against the wall. Like in the coalscuttle yesterday, or, puppies in a kennel, Thomas thought.

On the other side of the armoire, they could hear Cohen's anxious voice.

"Oh, do not go upstairs yet. We haven't finished the final details of our arrangement. The boy can wait," Cohen snickered. "He may be easier to manage if he is tired."

Thomas shuddered.

"What makes you so interested in my plans for the native lad?" Mr James, drawled.

"There are as many different ways to sin as there are people in the world," Cohen answered briskly. "The Talmud is a complex book. Besides, I tend to prefer to take my pleasures with the natives. Boys and girls, I'm not fussy. As long as they are young."

Mr James laughed. "Well, he's outside for the night in the stables. We've had him shovelling horse manure to teach him to mind his tongue. You're welcome to him if you want. But I wouldn't go near him until he has had a good bath if I were you."

"I'll bear that in mind," Cohen said levelly. "Perhaps tomorrow, before you leave. But now, what will you really be doing with him? I'm not a fool, James. I keep my ear to the ground. If the Waikato tribes were really starting up their own boarding school and seeking Pākehā teachers I would have been the first to hear of it."

Mr James tapped his nose. The effort made him rock slightly, and Thomas began to worry that the unsteady drunkard might collapse and discover them behind the armoire. "A direct request from Governor Grey. Very important package. To be delivered safely. Matua is just a boy. Not of any importance in his own right. Disposable, you might say. But his father needs to be – better controlled."

Matua gave a stifled cry.

Mr James peered suspiciously around. "What was that?"

They both breathed as shallowly and slowly as they could. Fortunately, it seemed the alcohol had dulled Mr James's senses. After a moment, he returned to the topic at hand. "Forget I spoke. Come on, Cohen, are you sure you can be trusted with the Empire's secrets? You Jews have foreign brethren everywhere, are you for the Queen or against her?" He burped, noisily. "I mean it is one thing to share a, private proclivity for the young. But this is politics. Can you be trusted? Can you swear secrecy and mean to keep it? I have heard Jews break their vows – once a year, in the temple –"

Cohen made reassuring noises about Kol Nidre being an old ceremony of no import and offered to buy Mr James another drink to show good faith. They wandered off unsteadily, back to the bar.

"Now. Quick." Thomas ran to the door. Behind him, he saw Matua hesitate, and look inside the cigar-smoked saloon. "Are you mad?"

"I want to find out what's going on. I want to find out what he intends to do with me." Matua jutted out his chin. "It's something about my father."

Thomas took a deep breath. "If you don't come right now, I am going to scream for that bastard to come and rescue me from you. And then we will both be damned."

Matua sullenly followed him across the threshold.

Outside, the hotel shed light onto the muddy ground. Beside it, the night sky sparkled faintly like a woman's necklace. They stepped away from the tavern as quickly as they could, and immediately great white clouds of milky light splashed across the dark above. A drunken Pākehā saw them go and shouted a rude joke about the friendship between a donkey and a horse. They ignored him, and hurried onwards towards the river.

The settlement was busy. Well-dressed settlers passed them, fiddling with pocketwatches and carrying week-old newspapers that had been horse-and-steamered down from Auckland. They were earnestly discussing the merits of the various plots of land that the local Māori were offering to sell. It was generally agreed that they were swampish and poor quality, and it might be better to wait to invest until Grey and his men had shown the measure of British power in the district. Surely then the Māori would learn the folly of trying to haggle for high prices, and stop keeping the best farming land for themselves.

Behind them came other Europeans, with worn clothes and haggard eyes. They did not talk about investments but carried all their belongings in a sack and whispered to each other about where might be the safest place to camp. Thomas ached with windswept longing for the past as he heard the a sound of his tongue. He had spoken it at home in the bogland but here in New Zealand his father and mother had announced they would no longer use it, it being a derelict primitive relic, of no use in this modern cosmopolitan country. "You won't forget it," they told him. But he knew he already was.

Then at last they came to the great river. Under the largest of the pohutakawa, there was the little boat, just as the stablehands had promised. There too was a group of Māori warriors, taking a night's rest from the exhausting labour of digging trenches on the hill. Did they know that in Ireland some hills were also strange-shaped, with ditches and ramparts, but they had been dug by the fairies, the Sidhe, not by men? Perhaps that was where Pa warfare had started, at home amongst the Sidhe.

They climbed into the boat. For the first time, Matua looked uncertain. "I hadn't thought of where we should go. You can go home, but I can't. The Reverend Simpson will just have me kidnapped again. But I don't know where to go without falling into the hands of Governor Grey and his men."

"South, to the King movement?"

Matua bit his lip. "I'm not sure they would welcome me. I think they think my father is too friendly towards the British. They call him one of the Queenies."

Thomas thought of the Irish back home. The painfully

thin neighbours that grew weaker and weaker over years, then disappeared to die into their homes. The terrible years that had killed all four of his grandparents, and weakened his little brother so much that he never recovered his health when it was over. Ended up dying of some ship fever on the way here. "I know. We'll go north," he said. "But not to Auckland, to Onehunga, where the ships dock from Britain and Ireland." Joy stirred in him, as he remembered the familiar accents and white cob cottages where he had landed. "They've settled retired soldiers there, to try to act as a barrier." Between Auckland and the Waikato, between you and me, he thought. "But they've made a mistake, in my opinion, because they're mainly Irish. The Fencibles, they're called."

Matua shrugged. In his opinion, whatever wars they'd fought at home the Europeans all stuck together once they got out here.

"Well, we can try. But don't get your hopes up. I've been selling fish at the barracks, remember? And I tell you, most of the soldiers Grey's bringing out to fight us are Irish too."

Thomas shook his head. (Young, I was back then you see. I didn't know the cruelty of the world. Yet again poor Matua had to educate me. And not for the last time).

"You blind sprat." He spat, just missing Thomas' foot. "They might not love your Queen, but they hate us more."

"That can't be true. The poor of the world, we stick together. That's what my father says."

"Oh yeah? Well, guess what my father says. He says the Irish and the Scots are going to be worse than the Tommies, once the battle starts. He says you Celts've collected all the shit the English laid on you over the years and dumped it out on us."

2019

Hamilton

Adele and Ben have been sitting together in the hospital for hours. By the time they arrived, Ben was feeling a little better. That meant, when the triage nurse asked him if he could remember what had happened, he could tell them: he had had a sudden and inexplicable urge to harm himself, he had wanted to jump in front of a car or slash his wrists. Because he wasn't sure that was a good idea, he had simply sat down in front of the motel and waited until he felt better.

After that, things happened very fast. He was whisked in a wheelchair to a private room where the nurse gave him a hospital gown to wear and apologetically confiscated all his belongings and clothes. That meant that everyone saw the partially healed slashes on his arms. Rosemary burst into soft sniffling tears and Adele wished she had said something to someone sooner.

The duty psychiatrist would be here shortly, the nurse said.

It was all so impossible, thought Adele. Ben just wasn't the kind of person to do this to himself. He was too laidback, too thoughtful. But what did she know what it was like being him on the inside? She thought often that she was a worthless piece of shit. You would never know that by speaking to her. Not even Cynthia knew much about that. All the Family Court mess, and all about her. She caused so much trouble, sometimes it felt like it would be better if she didn't exist.

Ben started to spasm again. His jerks were so violent this time it looked like he might fall off the bed. The nurse rushed to put up the rails. Then she pressed a big red button over the bed, like in all the science fiction movies, Adele thought. She gripped it with one hand, holding Ben's splaying arm with the other. After about ten seconds, he shuddered, and was still.

Nurses and doctors ran into the cubicle from across the department. They attached wires to Ben's chest. An ECG, Adele could identify it from Shortland Street. They must be really worried about it then. Oh look, they were monitoring his breathing now too.

A different nurse came and sat, watching the numbers on his machines, at the end of the bed. She didn't do anything, but just having her there was comforting.

"It's demons, isn't it." Rosemary spoke flatly.

"No," answered the nurse, forcefully. "This is a health issue. He's had a seizure of some kind."

"A seizure? Like a convulsion?"

"Yes, that's right."

"He had some of those when he was younger. The demons got into him."

"Oh, right." Adele watched the nurse ask, in a carefully neutral tone: "and what did you do about them?"

"Well, we were going to take him to the doctor, but then the pastor said to try prayer. So we prayed for deliverance, and miraculously they went away. I mean, they went on for a while. A few years. But he was delivered of evil. He's been a good boy since then."

"When did he have the last – demon?" the nurse enquired with a tactful frown.

"Last year."

"And he's never seen a doctor."

"No."

"Did it ever happen at school? Did anyone tell you he should see a doctor?"

"Well no," Rosemary spoke clearly, but her eyes were evasive. "None of them have been anything like as bad as this."

They sat for hours, sipping lukewarm coffee in polystyrene cups. Ben felt better at points, but then he would have another seizure, and Rosemary would start to cry again.

Cynthia and Sheila turned up with Mark. By now it was well past midnight. Early dawn, really. Adele could see a pale sliver of light on the distant horizon from the kitchen window where she went to make a coffee. They all stood awkwardly around in a supportive huddle, whilst Mark tried to talk to the nurse about what the Talmud said about pubes. It was all very like being in the campervan. For a moment, Adele felt as if this afternoon hadn't happened, and everything was going to be all right.

"Excuse me, are you Mrs Cynthia Murphy?"

Cynthia didn't even bother looking up, she was so busy comforting her friend.

"Yes, that's right, can I help you?"

Adele looked across, wondering idly who would know her mother's name in hospital. Then she flinched. The strange man from the beach and the marae, that was who. Only now he was wearing a shirt and tie, and carrying some papers with an air of authority.

"And can I ask you to identify your daughter, Adele Wairere Smith?"

This time Cynthia looked up sharply. The voice was gravelly, formal, almost robotic. The man's eyes were little grey pebbles. No emotion. As if, as if, Adele thought wildly, he was not entirely real. He had been built from a kitset, in some cupboard somewhere, wheeled out for this occasion. That made sense. He had to be a robot. No one human could bear to do a job like this.

"Why? What do you want?"

The man gestured behind him. Two young police

officers, who were standing awkwardly in the corridor, gave sheepish nods.

"The Family Court has made an order for your daughter to be removed from your care on a without-notice basis."

Sheila looked up. "What? But that's ridiculous. That's only used in cases where the child's life is at risk."

"I have the paperwork here," the man went on, as if Sheila did not exist. "The judge made the order at about 6pm tonight. Her father is to have sole custody and you may have supervised contact until such time as a date is set for hearing –"

Cynthia did not move or speak. Adele tried to, but her mouth didn't seem to work properly. Like Ben, who was watching in silent but speechless horror from the bed. The man turned, and held the papers out to her. She took them, numbly. As she did her hands brushed his. She noticed that they were strangely cold.

"Give me that." Sheila grabbed the paperwork. "Where's the affidavit? What's the evidence? What have they accused her of?" She scanned the sheets and threw them on the floor. One of the policemen stooped to pick them up. She put her foot on them, hard, so he could not.

"Disgusting. I thought so. Cynthia, you've got to fight this. Your daughter's being taken away because you are exercising your right – your legal right - to home education. Oh, and you're not very good at tidying the house. And once or twice, before you had children, you took some drugs. And apparently that now constitutes neglect and serious risk. Because it's not a normal childhood. According to the Family Court. Or your ex-husband, which seems to amount to the same thing."

She looked up at the police officers. Her voice shook with fury. Righteous fury, Adele thought with the part of her brain that was still functioning. If Justice had a voice that is how it would sound. But it also sounded whirling and panicky, like the desperate thoughts of a terrified woman, who had just looked into the abyss of family separation, and seen it could happen to her too.

And there was an extra grate in her voice. A sort of squeezed silence. Like she was saying all this to cover up some else. The way a guilty person might, to deflect attention from her crime. But that was crazy, thought Adele, this is nothing to do with her. She hasn't done anything wrong.

"And you're taking a break from dealing with actual crime, family crime, I mean hasn't New Zealand got one of the biggest problems with domestic and sexual violence and all that stuff, you're going off duty from that, so you can come and do this, here, tonight?"

2019

Mangere Village

They came before dawn. Like the sneaky bastards they were, they snuck down from their base without warning. We'll leave you alone, if you stay in that field. No action overnight.

That's what they said.

But they didn't mean any of it, any more than their great-great-grandparents meant a word of the Tiriti. Like I said. They don't play by the rules, you see. Never do. It's no use being nonviolent when the other side mean war.

They'll play nice when they want, but they're full of lies. And like the poor saps we are, we fall for it. Again, and again, and again.

They came wearing dark clothes. No torches, no warning. Rippled into us like dirty water, ripped open the tents at the top of the field. Started carrying them, with people still asleep inside. Children screamed. Parents were screaming too. Then they started driving us back, off the ground, shouting. Herding us like a bunch of cattle, back towards the open road.

I'd been asleep. Or at least I think I was. Meant to be on guard duty by the back campfire. I was doing my bit, I tried to at least, but I drifted off sometime during an argument between two Ngāpuhi and a Ngāti Whaatu chicks about how much Ngāpuhi ancestry exactly you had to have to qualify for an iwi scholarship.

I woke up a bit later, put wood on the fire.

By that time they were friends and banging on together about how unfair it was that the dragonboating and the waka ama teams had to share funding and a coach at uni. Someone else interrupted to say that the waka that had been burnt in a Ngāpuhi raiding party a hundred years ago was still remembered by their iwi and since Ngāpuhi were getting close to a nice fat Tiriti payout, which would make them way richer than anyone else, was there any chance of paying compensation for that boat? In the corner was this old geezer who was groaning on about how we shouldn't be too proud of ourselves because we weren't tangata whenua really, when we'd shown up in the Aotearoa we'd wiped out a prior race of inhabitants called the Morori.

He was old and gentle, and no one had the heart to tell him that the Mooroori had only ever been on Chatham Island, they were probably part of the same Māori diaspora arrival, and he'd been fed a bunch of lies at Paakehaa school. Even I know that and I've failed every exam I've taken for six years. So yeah, I went back to sleep, and it wasn't until the screaming started that I saw what was happening. Morning mist and fluorescent jackets, they were quick enough to put those on once we'd clocked what was happening.

So we all stood toe to toe, staring up at the police officers in front of us. Some of them had the decency to look embarrassed. Others smirked. "If you're Pasifika or Māori, ask your boss not to be rostered here!" yelled one of the crowd. "And go home and read up on the dawn raids, because guess what, that's exactly the stunt you just tried to pull again here!" Three women brought up a huge flag. "Spread it out. Make them trample it if they want to take us."

There was crying and screaming, and one girl was in tears because her undies were in the tent and she couldn't get back to them. But me, I was a happy sod. Because you know why? I didn't know until then, what I'd do if they actually rushed us. I was afraid I'd lose control. Didn't have a knife, but I couldn't see how if a cop came heavy on me, how I wouldn't end up using my fists. You know what, the way they treat you in care, it's like they expect you to be a thug, you start by tryna prove everyone wrong, but you end up thinking, nah. What's the point, I'll just lean into it.

Reckon maybe part of me believed the stereotype too, that old shite about male Māori being naturally violent, Once Were Warriors, that kinda thing. Maybe I didn't think I had it in me to be anything else. But that morning I knew, they'd come and thumped us in the gut and I did what we wanted, stood up to them without losing my cool and thumping back. I was a protector. Non-violence, I could do it.

Great feeling.

Like I said, I'm not a spiritual type, but that moment I sorta reckoned that if Rongomataane was the sort of unlikely god of peace who actually existed, that he'd be pretty stoked with how I'd handled the whole thing . Trouble had come, and I'd nailed it. Stood there like a boss, let them roar and shout, and I held my ground and didn't give them any excuse to get me arrested. Didn't even swear. It felt great, I tell you. Yeah, a protector.

That's what I was.

And for a moment, I didn't even care about Thin-Lips, and finding out what he was doing now or where he lived.

But of course, that wasn't the end of it, the good moment when you love yourself and feel that maybe life is purposeful and not a piss-poor sadistic cosmic joke never lasts for long.

Because now we were at war, basically, and the police were watching us with narrow eyes, waiting for their next chance. And I didn't know how long it would last, and how brave I could be, and what would happen if they did lose their cool, accuse us of shit we hadn't done and drag us all down to the copshop. I was shitting myself when I thought about being locked up again. Like when – yeah, well, let's not go into that now.

So when some blood comes up and offers to take my place staring down the cop in front of me so I can have some breakfast and a pee, I'm all for it. I go down to the breakfast tent and whoa, there's the moko guy in leathers. He flings an arm around me and asks how I am.

"Chur, bro. Good."

"And your whanau? They weren't up in the field?"

I shake my head. No, I'm here on my own, bro. Thanks for asking. He nods, gives me a friendly punch on the arm. "Well, you need anyone to chat to, come along and hang with me." And he's off, back to take his turn on the field.

Oh, I get it. So now you're wondering, what about Mum and Sis? And my Nana, what about her? Far out. You didn't believe all that rot? All right. The bit with my Nana and the old taiaha, that our family lost, that much is true. She told me about it before I got taken away. But the rest, who knows? All my record says is that Mum was sent the date of the court hearing and she didn't appear. No one knows what happened to her after that.

But it's kinda weird and lonely being here at Ihumatao by myself. Worse even than leaving care, cause all the other Māori seem to have whanau and jeez, they look so happy with it. So is it so bad if I make out like I've got a family? It's not even like you're a real person. Just a stupid notebook.

So I'll quit pretending I've got whanau, and also quit pretending you're real. Like the cops that morning, they quit pretending too.

2019

Hamilton

"I'm not going with you. You can't make me." Adele looked at Thin-Lips, then across at the two police officers. They were young, spotty. Acne. Perhaps only three or four years older than her.

"Anyway, you've got no right to bring the police along. I haven't committed a crime."

Her voice was shaking with the fact that she knew she was talking shit. They would make her go with them if she messed them around. You didn't bring police officers along just for show. Playing for time, that's all she could do. Pointless, really, but you had to try.

They looked awkward. "Do you want to talk to her, Mr James?"

"No no. I was only hired by her father to keep an eye on them so we knew where to bring the uplift notice when he was granted. It's over to you now."

He spoke with satisfaction, as if rather enjoying their discomfiture with the task.

"Please," one of them said. "Don't upset your mother."

"We can do this the easy way or the hard way," his colleague added, as if reading lines from a bad police TV series. Adele almost giggled. Perhaps they meant to make her laugh, to break the tension and make her easier to handle. Funny man and stooge.

"It's a hospital, we don't want to upset the patients." That was true, Adele thought, but she and Cynthia mattered too.

She looked them up and down. They were strong and fit. She was neither. Homeschool sports and fitness group was, to be honest, rubbishy. (Although definitely not bad enough to be worth breaking up families). But with her couch potato habits and asthma, she wouldn't get far. Anyway, the police had been sensible enough to block the exits.

"Adele," said Cynthia suddenly, as if unfreezing. "Go with them. Please. It's not just about homeschooling. This is a big deal. "

Adele shook her head. "I won't. Not unless you tell me what's going on." Cynthia looked across at the police officers. "All right. Give me a moment, OK?"

The police officers didn't reply. Cynthia started to gabble, speaking so fast she could scarcely be understood.

"Other women go through this. Quite often, actually. Statistics show it. The more women who report domestic violence, the more likely they are to lose their children to their father. It's crazy, really, New Zealand has the worst domestic violence statistics in the developed world, but somehow we've got to the situation where the courts think that the woman who complains is the problem. Parental Alienation syndrome, they call it. It's a discredited scientific theory and nowhere else do the courts still take it seriously, except here."

Across the hallway, a grandmother who was recovering from a suspected heart attack sat up to get a better view of what was going on. Cynthia raised her voice slightly, so the whole ward could hear.

"They really will take you and we won't be together for a while. It's my fault. I should have told you what your father was threatening. He's got Oranga Tamariki on his side. Nothing to do with homeschooling, really. They're just using that as an excuse. You know the family violence advocacy I've been doing? That's the problem. They said they would take you if I didn't stop, I didn't believe them, but here we are. It is for real. It's been going on for months.

They say I'm putting you off your father. Please. Go quietly. I don't want my last sight of you to be in handcuffs."

What could you say? What could you do?

What Mum asked, that was what.

She shrugged. "Whatever."

"Do you want to give Mum a kiss?" one of the police officers asked.

She shrugged again. "Yeah, nah, yes all right."

"You'll see her soon." That was a lie, they all knew that.

She kissed her politely on the cheek, the way they never did, and headed for the door with the police as if they were her new best friends. She even turned and gave Cynthia a final, cheery wave. Once she was far enough away that she reckoned her mum wouldn't see the tears stinging her eyes.

You always wonder how you will react when the worst happens. Maybe it was the shock, but Adele found that at the worst moment of her life, she was entirely calm. No time to emote. She had to get away.

Choosing the right moment was important. They must be far away enough from the hospital that Cynthia couldn't see them from the window. But it must be before she could be put in a car. So she dawdled until Police Officer Acne opened the back door of the waiting police car – "they've sent you an actual police car, that could be used to arrest real troublemakers," she could imagine the disgusted tone in Sheila's voice - and gestured her inside.

That was her final chance, and when she made the inevitable, futile, pointless, important run for it. Up towards the road. Crazy, really, where did she think she was going to go? Perhaps she wasn't thinking so clearly after all.

They caught her, of course, and she fought and bit and scratched in a most unladylike manner until they threw her to the ground and put her in handcuffs, just like a proper criminal. "Proper little Māori chick, isn't she?" Acne said to Tall and Thin, whilst she was still lying on the ground. They laughed.

"Pasifika kids are the worst. Butter wouldn't melt in their mouth when they're with their parents, it's all respect the elders and aiga, then you get them on their own and little devils the lot of them."

They took her back to the police car quite quickly after that, and checked in on the police radio. "Yes, we've picked her up, bit of resistance but nothing major, she's calm now." That's what you think, thought Adele. "It's quite a drive to where we've got to deliver you, do you want us to buy you a Big Mac on the way?" asked Tall and Thin.

"I don't eat Big Macs, they're unhealthy," Adele sniffed in her best imitation of Cynthia. "And bad for the environment." Actually, she was rather partial to fast food on occasion, but she was feeling contrary and her head was sore where they had banged it on the ground. She thought it was probably accidental, but it had all happened too fast to be sure.

Tall and Thin whistled. "Suit yourself." He turned into the drive-in and ordered a couple of Meals. The frozen Coke made a loud slurping noise as he drank it. A loud burp.

"Ah, that's it."

"Like a piss when you need it, better than sex," Acne sniggered.

And school is supposed to teach me socialisation, Adele thought bitterly.

"Do your mothers know you speak like that at work?" she asked.

Acne said nothing and glared at her, wiping his bloody nose. At least he'll know he was beaten up by a girl, thought Adele with satisfaction. But it didn't really help. She looked out of the window and watched the closed shops. Shuttered like her, pretending not to care. The past ten years since they left her dad felt suddenly like a delightful, magical dream. Now she was awake, and the world was terrifying again.

"Wanna listen to some music?"

Why not. She nodded, and they turned on the car radio. It was on the hour, but a commercial station, so only a few seconds of news.

Tensions are rising at Ihumatao....a dawn raid, crowds refuse to leave the field... Amnesty International visit the site, and state they have concerns about the escalation....police superintendent reports that one of his Asian officers was racially abused and told to go home...now to politics, the United Nations have yet again called upon the New Zealand government to set up a Royal Commission into the abuse of women by the Family Court....

Same old, same old. She'd been hearing all this for years. She tried to take comfort in the thought of Acne's battered nose and rapidly blackening eye. Sometimes it's not so important that you win a fight, as that you dared to try. You had to cling not just to the successes in life, but to the brave attempts, when you threw everything you got at the invader, and didn't win. Otherwise, how could the Ihumatao crowd know the bitter history, and still find the guts to try again?

She'd have to do the same. If she was going to get away.

1862

Bombay Hills

Matua insisted that they took the river north. Thomas didn't want to. His head still ached, and even the gentle rock of a rowing boat brought on a rush of nausea.

Also, the Great South Road would be quick. It wasn't straight like the ones the Romans had built to suppress Celtic Britain, but nor was it as eccentrically winding as the country tracks Thomas remembered from back home. Crossing from his village to Wexford Town was like following a long coil of rope, or – as Mr James might have put it – a man's guts. Quicker to go over the hills.

But the Great South Road was different. Designed for armies, not peasants. An

efficient system of transport for goods and beasts.

"It's not the Great South Road anyway," Matua protested when he suggested it.

"It goes north."

Thomas rolled his eyes. "It doesn't matter."

"It does."

Matua sucked on his lip and wondered whether to bother trying to explain. Language wasn't just words, it was also people and life. He'd seen it happening all around him. You gave way on the small things like names and then suddenly you were drowning in European words. It didn't happen the other way around. You never heard a Pakeha speak the Great Fish of Maui, for example, or Matariki. They just said North Island and the Pleiades. Sometimes he worried that the Māori were getting so keen on English words and concepts that they would start to forget their own speech. That would be like losing their whole place in the universe, because there were so many concepts that simply didn't exist anywhere else. Even colours, how could the English not see that puruu-poouri and oorangi and kahurangi meant different things? They were not all blue. If you could not trust them to see with their own eyes, how could you trust their language to contain the whole world?

His father reassured him that was ridiculous. Of course the Māori would never let their language die out, any more than they would come under British military control.

Although Thomas had a point. Whatever you called it, the Great Road was the

quickest and easiest way north. But that was also its disadvantage, because it was so wellknown. And without an adult accompanying them, they'd look conspicuous.

"Too easy for people to remember us when that bastard comes asking. And then

we're done for. He'll never let us get away a second time."

Thomas remembered Mr James' thin lips under hard pebble eyes, and the cold clamminess of his hands. He shuddered a little at the thought. "Yeah."

So they rowed the boat up the quiet river towards Mercer, and then headed west towards the small settlement of Tuakau. That would add another day to their journey, but worth it, Matua thought, if it lengthened the gap between them and Mr James if they had to join the road.

"We'll cross back to Pokeno tomorrow. If anyone asks I'm selling fish."

Afterwards, Thomas could never quite remember how they had found food on the way. There had been berries, yes, and a few fish they had speared with sticks in the river. He also had an odd memory of falling asleep on the bank and having a dream of a woman kissing him tenderly. When he woke, there was a loaf of bread. For the rest of his life, he could never quite work out if that was a natural event, or the kind of hallucination you have when you're hungry and have been hit on the head, or if, as it felt at the time, he'd been visited by one of the Faery.

It was on the evening of the third day that they came up towards the Pokeno roadworks. Thomas knew this area better than Matua, who had never been to Auckland itself. It felt good to be the expert for once. "We've got to keep off the road itself as much as possible," he explained, "not just because we might be spotted, but because we don't have any money for the tollhouses. When we came down four years ago, it was mud all the way from Drury, you had to take a canoe even to get to here. The milestones stopped way up north. Now there's two thousand and a half men working day and night on the road."

" Māori ?"

Thomas shook his head. "Soldiers, all of them. Battlehardened. They've all fought

in India or Taranaki. Pa says they're spoiling for a fight. Really hate the " – he bit back the word.

"They really hate unfinished roads, right?" Matua's tone was dry. Thomas squirmed.

"Can you hear that?"

In the distance, a bugle sounded. It shattered the peaceful evening like hailstones flattening the winter grass at home. I say home, but where is my home now? Thomas wondered. Is home where we come from, or where we dream of, or where we somehow end up? Or perhaps it's not where we live at all, but where we die and are buried. Which means that my brother's home is in that horrible little grave in Onehunga, just outside the Fencible village. I hope we can get there, I'd like to go and say hello to him again.

Maybe we're only really at home when we are dead.

Matua heard the sound with a shiver. It had an unearthly tone. When you blow a

reed through your fingers, and you get the angle just

right, it shrieks like a kehua spiritghost. That was how the bugle rang. It was hollow but shrill, like the church bell that Reverend Simpson had imported at great expense from Australia. Deathly, Matua thought.

That bugle is like the cry of the wairua when an animal is bludgeoned to death for food.

Now there were drums, crashing in the distance as if they expected to drill through the earth by sound. Twittering flutes accompanied them. Neither of the boys had ever heard a fife, but for Thomas it was delightfully reminiscent of the tin whistle. He didn't play much, but he loved the sound of the whistle and fiddle together on the boat.

Matua loved Māori flutes as much as he did wrestling. His mother was a skilled player. She would let him sit at her feet whilst she let the goddess Raukatauri dance in her moth-shape inside the music she made, promising him that one day he would learn and like Raukatauri, never be parted from it. He had learnt. It had been hard at first, as all the traditional skills were, but he'd persevered until gradually his hands had softened to the work and the putarino reedmusic had become his third language. He would have that forever, he'd thought, like Māori at home and speaking English with Thomas. But now he was on the run, and his flute was at home, and he ached for it, and wished his mother had not told him untruths. You did lose music too, when you lost your whanau and home.

It didn't take long for the military band to fade into the distance. Must be the end of the working day for the roadbuilders. They walked on. A muddy stream, hardly worth the bother of taking your shoes off for. Not like the Mangatawhiri Stream to the southeast, which also looked small and insignificant but was in fact a powder keg. When the Māori had elected their own King a few years earlier, he had declared that stream the limit of British power. It ran just above Meremere, and if the British crossed it, there would be immediate war.

"Now don't you go getting your feet wet. We've got a way to go before camp." Just ahead of them, a British voice. One of those posh ones, that belonged to an officer or a reverend. Matua and Thomas looked at each other in alarm, and simultaneously hit the ground.

"Are you sure we will be welcome? We haven't got the boy." The other voice was also that of a grandee, but younger, and more nervous. "Grey and Cameron will not take no for an answer."

"Oh no, definitely not. We'll wait for James to deliver the package to Pokeno before we head any further north."

"Will he do it? What if he lets us down? He's a couple of days late."

"James will do whatever we ask." The older voice chuckled. "He knows how im-

portant the little package of native shit is to our plans. Governor Grey has offered him the headmastership of that new reformatory they are building in Panmure. No one will care what he does to the young delinquents. It's not like the east Auckland settlements, where they're holding meetings calling for his blood. So Grey can wield both stick and carrot. Any trouble, and he'll turn Mr James over to them. Those parents will break every bone in his body and drop him off the St Heliers cliffs."

The voices were getting closer. Thomas pressed his nose down into the ground.

"We're nearly there. The Khyber Pass, the locals are calling this section now. Because of the fear of Māori attack. I must say, I'm rather proud of the propaganda we've done in this regard. The Māori have totally respected our boundary and yet we've managed to convince the locals that they are constantly on the point of sacking the whole city. When we get our hands on the little brown turd –"

Then it happened. A loud unexpected sound from Matua. The two spies stiffened and pounced.

Such rotten luck, he always said bitterly afterwards.

Tane, the god of the woods must have had it in for him, perhaps there were too many occasions when he had been out birdnesting with Thomas the European way without making the proper karakia. Why, they'd even blown eggs together for Thomas' sister's collection. Taking the gifts of the forest for their own. Not to eat or wear, but shut up in a lifeless box. No Māori tohunga would approve of that.

As he lay on the wet ground, once again feeling the jerk of his arms being roughly tied being his back, Matua sweated with fear. Not of the Paakehaa, but the gods. So much time and care he'd spent, following the rules. And yet it wasn't enough. He'd cursed himself with those beautiful blue eggshells they'd spent hours collecting together on Port Waikato cliffs. Horrible to think how such a delicate and fragile object could cause so much harm.

Afterwards, Thomas tried to convince him that he wasn't doomed, that the sound he'd made was of obvious natural origin. But Matua knew better. It wasn't as if he had given his belly and bum much food with which to make music. But the loud patero happened, and it was loud and musical and unmistakable. The two Queen's soldiers thought it was hilarious that the little brown turd they had been trying to capture had betrayed himself into their hands by a loud fart.

2019

Mangere Bridge

Thin-Lips was back. Typical maggot behaviour, he only came out when the world was turned to rotten shit.

He wasn't hanging around with his police mates, now, either. No, he'd mingled in with the protestors. You couldn't stop anyone coming, that was the difficult part of managing an event like this.

Now the dawn raid had hit the news. Impossible to think that there were even more dudes who wanted to join us, but there were.

There was going to be a concert this weekend, and the crowd was swelling. Everyone was showing up, from Māori children's TV presenters to Green MPs. At least now the police had realised they were sitting on a public relations nightmare. There'd been urgent phone calls from Wellington. They'd obviously been told to take a back seat.

I decided that with all these rich stiffs showing up, it was time to take a few days'

break from cleaning the loos. So I did kitchen duty instead. It's a good place to hang out if you don't have anyone you know to talk to.

I'm not a great chef, but you don't need to be to boil a tub of water for noodles

and chop veg. It was chill, sorta relaxing. And I like when I'm, you know, it's the kind of work I enjoy. No one bossing you and making you try to look manly. Cleaning and housework, that's always where I feel at home.

I used to think it was cause I missed my mum.

Now I'm outta the system, and doing more on my own. I realised, it's not her. Or it's not just that. It's me. Not just housework either. Lipstick too. Nail polish. I liked all of that, and to be honest I wasn't quite sure why. I mean, I was a guy, right? So what was all this?

One of the nice things about Ihumatao was, we were all muffled up in fleece and gumboots. You could hardly tell from the outside what anyone had inside their pants. I dunno why, but it was kind of a relief. Like the rest of life was all in a straightjacket, and somehow without realising it, you'd taken it off. Weird, man. Or chick, or whatever it wasn't obvious that you were any more.

So this old nana comes up and watches me work. All right, she's not that old. Maybe forty, forty-five? But it was hard to tell, because she'd obviously had a rough life. Her face was all tattered and torn, and she had one of those broken teeth at the front, you know? Obviously spent some time on meth. She comes up all friendly like.

"Hey, buddy. Kia kaha. I just wanted to say, you're doing a great job. Saw you scrubbing the toilets yesterday too. Bet your mum is proud. Hope so."

I dunno what to say, so I give up a fistbump. A slight electric hits as she bumps

me back. Like we had, you know, a connection. Girl power. Not that I'm a girl, right, but whatever, it was cool. Like the news we got later, that government had told everyone to stand back, cool it, stop the building, and negotiate. It wasn't a win, but it was a good start.

So of course leadership upped the ante. Why not? Nothing to lose, we were al-

ready all over the international news.

"Come and see us, Jacinda."

Those were the signs they were painting outside. They wanted Jacinda to come and see Ihumatao, decide for herself. But she never showed. Everyone else did, though.

It was like being in a TV studio. Cameras everywhere you turned. I swear, we were celebs. People came for all sorts of reasons, and not all of them were good. Turned out that's why frontline leader was barefoot. It was because some cheeky sod had broken into his tent, taken his Bible and his shoes.

So I wasn't surprised to see Thin-Lips show up, snaking his way through the

crowd. If he wanted to cause trouble, this was the place.

I was holding this big butchers' knife, chopping potatoes like a boss. I held it close for a moment. He was on his own. Wandering through the crowd. I might not have a better chance.

But we were winning, for now at least. Didn't want to wreck it. No, not today. ThinLips could wait. If he thought there was prey to be found onsite, he'd be back. Also, the signs had made me think. It would kind of be cool to meet Jacinda. And if Ihumatao became a murder site, she'd definitely never show up.

1860

Meremere

The Redoubt was still under construction. It would be a great fort soon, and the plan was that it contain twenty seven huts, a parade ground and a hospital. The defensive ditches had been dug and were bigger than any European fort that had ever been built in New Zealand. But for now, the inside was still a mess of tents and half-built structures. Over four hundred men were already living there, but without proper facilities their red coats were mudstained and the latrine holes stank.

It was evening when they arrived. Thomas and Matua walked in front of the two spies, who were eloquently triumphant to everyone they met about their capture. Matua, being the important package, had his hands tied: his head was covered with a bag like, Thomas realised with a chill in his guts, the kind a hangman might use. Thomas was tied to him with one hand, which meant he could guide him. The other hand was attached to a soldier. As if they were pet dogs.

It didn't look like things at the Redoubt would be improve soon. Apparently a group of contractors had just refused to deliver wood that was needed for the huts and ramparts. It had rained a lot in recent weeks, and the southern road which was not yet metalled had become so muddy and impassable they had given up and returned home. All this Thomas and Matua learnt from the heated conversations that took place between the sentries that guarded the camp and the spies who had captured and delivered them.

The spies had been expecting bounty and praise. In fact they got the opposite. Governor Grey and Cameron might be prepared to pay handsomely for whoever delivered Matua to the British Army ("Why?" thought Matua to himself, his head fuzzing with the bewilderment of it all. "Why am I suddenly so important?") But that was the perspective in Auckland, where old men peered at maps and made secret political plans in darkened rooms.

Out here on the frontier, Thomas and Matua were a nuisance, because they had nowhere to keep them yet. Of course, eventually the new fort would have a small jailhouse. Just a couple of cells, to keep dissolute soldiers and significant packages until they could be transferred to Auckland. But without the wood, all work had stopped. Matua wondered if they were planning to take a lot of mystery prisoners, or whether they would build the jailhouse just for him.

There had been just enough timber to string together poles in a row. They stalked oddly across the landscape, like the stone milestones Thomas had seen in Ireland and on the Great South Road. In Ireland the milestones were cut by desperate fathers on famine relief, pointless work in exchange for bread. Control of the poor. Here they were hewn by stonemasons under orders from the military, to make it easier to lay out the road. Different reason, different craftsmen, but the same reason at bottom. Power, control. These poles were not like that, though, they were much taller, closer together and also had wires strung between them. Birds sat on top of them, the pretty sparrows that were being imported from England to render this land more palatable to Europeans. Thomas wondered what on earth was the point of building these new birds artificial branches, when New Zealand had so many perfectly good trees.

They sat on the ground and waited. After about an hour

of desultory argument between the scouts and sentries as to whose responsibility it was to take the package to Governor Grey and what might be done with Thomas – there seemed several options, including giving him a sound thrashing and sending him home, or enlisting him as a drummer boy – a loud Scottish voice called them to attention.

"All right, all right. Move along. I'll handle them from here. My goodness, what a sorry pair. Take that bag off his head, he's not a sack of potatoes."

Light flooded Matua's eyes as the black bag was removed. Oh no, he thought, I'm going to cry again, and then Thomas will be convinced forever I'm a cissy. He tried to distract himself by looking around. The size and scale of the Redoubt was overwhelming, even more so than the light in his eyes. A sinking recognition hit his stomach. My father's been wrong all along, he thought, he was so sure after Hone Heke saw them off in Northland and the mess that they made in Taranaki that the British wouldn't want to risk another war here.

But no one would be building a fort like this on the border of our country if their intent was peace. It's not just a defensive garrison, it's a city. You could hold a whole army here and send them out to attack day after day, week after week. Years, even. And the road north to make sure you were well supplied, whatever the weather. No wonder our own troops are working so hard to fortify Meremere. They've sent scouts north, to see what is going on. Yes, we are going to be in battle against each other. It's only a matter of time.

The Sergeant Major threw the black bag disdainfully on the ground. "Don't need that. I'm not afraid of you looking at me. Let's have a dekkie, now, shall we?"

His joints cracked, as he knelt down, eyes twinkling slightly. Thomas found he rather liked the look of him. Against all the odds, Matua had a sudden sense of safety.

Perhaps not home, but not quite in enemy hands.

"You two. Sight for sore eyes. Don't look like terrible enemies of Her Majesty to me."

He introduced himself. "Sergeant-Major Blunt. Blunt by name, and blunt by nature. Which is good news for you boys, because although my sword is regulation sharp I don't like using it on prisoners."

His title was Quartermaster, he explained, which pretty much meant everything except actually fighting anyone. "Blankets and bedbugs and bandages and bully beef. That's my speciality." He would be in charge of the camp jail when it had actually been built, he explained, so it seemed only reasonable to take charge of them now. They were the first prisoners to be brought to Queen's Redoubt, and he hoped they would be well-behaved so that it was a pleasant experience for them all three. To be honest, looking at the pair of them, it looked as if what they needed most of all was food, and perhaps a decent bath. Would that do, for tonight?

Thomas and Matua nodded gratefully.

Then it would be arranged. They could be guarded in a tent and live quite the life of comfort for a day or so, while they waited for the new telegraph to send them instructions from Auckland. He didn't know what the instructions would be, but he would make sure he told them as soon as he knew. Then he would send them on their way, trusting to Gore and Good Queen Victoria. He was sure they would be well taken care of, even if he didn't quite himself understand why it had been necessary to capture such young and scrawny-looking boys. Matua asked what a telegraph was, and if it was faster than a message-runner. One of the sentries kicked him, hard, and told him to mind his tongue. "Stop that immediately," Serjeant-Major Blunt snapped, "he's in my custody now and we treat him well unless we've got a good reason to do otherwise."

The sentry regarded him balefully, but stepped back. "He's our prisoner, sir. He should show us respect."

"The British Empire plays fair. On the cricket pitch and in soldiering. Untie their hands. They can't eat dinner like that."

The sentry did so, reluctantly, pulling the ropes as harshly as he dared.

"Done. With respect, sir, were you in the Indian campaigns?"

"I was, and in my opinion we'd have saved ourselves a deal of trouble by treating the Sepoys better in the first place so they had no need to rise up. If you're going to have an Empire, treat your subject peoples well. A man doesn't risk his life for freedom unless the alternative has become unbearable."

"Isn't that treason, sir?"

"No, thanks to Good Queen Victoria and the British Parliament we have the blessing of free speech, and I like to use it. Patriotism means daring to tell the truth about the country you love. So keep your boots and fists to yourself. I won't have ill-treatment of any prisoner in this camp."

Water was brought, and some soup. No, not soup, Thomas realised as he put it to his mouth, beef stew. It tasted decent. Soldier rations, Thomas supposed. He knew the British Empire fed its troops well. They had to. An army marched on its stomach, or something like that, someone had said so. Father Murphy had told them about it in a sermon once. Of course you mustn't be too fond of earthly food, he had added, the only true nourishment was in heaven, but, well, he'd laughed, it's important to enjoy what Our Lord provides on this level of existence too. Munching now, Thomas felt that heavenly food could not be anywhere near as blissful as this.

"Don't eat too much, lads. If you haven't had much for a few days you'll throw it up." Sergeant-Major Blunt watched them with care. "If you hold that down, in an hour you can have some army biscuits. Sent all the way from Waitemata. I might even manage to find a bit of fruit cake."

Just when you had become determined to hate the British Army, Matua thought ruefully, they sent someone along who was prepared to look after you. He tangata he tangata he tangata. People were still people, no matter what side they were on.

"I wouldn't waste good food on them if I were you." One of the scouts who had brought them in lit his pipe and was waving it ostentatiously at the soldier. Ash floated down on them both. Like a warning of an eruption, thought Matua, thinking of the stories he had heard of mountains that exploded unexpectedly, now and again. Falling ash first, and then the terror of fire from the sky. War, volcanoes. Death came all the same. "And for your information, I am a first lieutenant, of significantly higher rank than yourself, so I suggest you listen to me."

Serjeant Major Blunt squared his shoulders and looked at the officer spy. "They will eat while they are with me, sir, exactly the same food as I and my men do. That's what I did with our prisoners of war in India, and that's what I will do here."

"Really? I wouldn't advise that approach here if I were you. The Sepoys were brave and cunning. And fond of reprisals, and outnumbered us by millions, so it made sense to give them few excuses to massacre. Here we are already the majority. We can be bold. Beside, New Zealand natives are of a different type. Primitive and brutish. Dogs don't sleep in beds, Sergeant, if you want to remain their masters."

"Sir, with respect. It is only reasonable to treat the other side the way that we would ourselves want to be treated if we were taken prisoner. There are discussions, even now, taking place in Geneva – there is talk of producing an agreement between nations for the care of prisoners and the wounded – a kind of international Convention –"

"If such a convention ever existed, which I doubt, it would never apply to prisoners of different races." He poked Matua's foot contemptuously. "We are not bound to treat those cursed descendants of Ham with the same gentle affection we might reserve for one of our own."

"Some might see differently, sir. Some might say we are all descended from monkeys, or even fossil fish, and the differences between the races are merely cosmetic."

The lieutenant snorted. With a slow deliberate movement, he reached for the closest sentry's bayonet. He took it, and pointed it directly at Sergeant-Major Blunt's stomach.

"And how does a mere sergeant major become so well informed in science and international affairs?"

"I have no children, sir, and I do not drink. All my pay goes on books. I have recently received a copy of *Origin of Species* from my mother in Edinburgh, and before that she sent me the *Communist Manifesto*. I teach myself, to the best of my ability, and I do all I can to encourage my men to do the same."

The lieutenant nudged the bayonet point a little bit closer, so that it threatened to tear the red fabric of his regimental jacket. Thomas was torn between a desire to cover his eyes, and a horrid sense of duty to watch what happened next.

"That is the kind of answer a foreign spy might give. We are in Auckland and the last posting for this regiment was Delhi. How do you know what is happening in Geneva?"

A small crowd of men gathered around him. He raised his voice, relishing the drama. "Dangerous elements are calling for the formation of an international commission to meddle with independent nations' conduct in wartime. This is obviously a threat to our country and must be resisted."

The bayonet jabbed. Sergeant Major Blunt stood very still. His jacket was now torn, and you could see the pale flesh underneath. Like Reverend Simpson, thought Thomas, only less hairy. Was that only a few days ago?

The watching men murmured. The Lieutenant continued his speech, as if addressing a political rally. But they're not on your side, Thomas thought. You're attacking someone they like.

" Her Majesty's government has been very concerned about it and is making urgent representations behind the scenes that this idea of the Red Cross, as I understand it is provisionally termed, should be immediately dropped. But this was not generally known in New Zealand. We discussed it – " he lowered his voice, theatrically – "at Kawau House, but the feeling was that the Māori might be emboldened by hearing of such fanciful ideas. Hence there has been nothing about it in the *Southern Cross.*" He swung around. "What have you to say to this, Quartermaster?"

Sergeant Major's voice shook, but he stood his ground. "Last year I read the book by Mr Durant about the terrible suffering on all sides at the Battle of Solférino. He states very clearly there what his suggestions are to remedy them. I was interested, and requested my mother send me newspaper clippings on the subject. It may not be public knowledge here in New Zealand, but the matter is being discussed widely in Edinburgh periodicals."

The men whistled and clapped. Sergeant Major Blunt, it was clear, was a popular man amongst the troops. With slight uncertainty, the lieutenant lowered the bayonet, as if suddenly realising he was surrounded on three sides. A coward, then, who didn't fancy his chances. Matua spat in disgust. Any real leader would have had the mana to hold his ground.

There was now a boisterous defiance in the Sergeant's tone. As if he knew he was winning, and was beginning to enjoy himself.

"My duty remains to treat these prisoners according to the law and my conscience. If you have a problem with that, take it up with the commanding officer of this Redoubt, or General Cameron."

The lieutenant looked at the watching men, and fingered his bayonet. A petulant look crossed his face. He stepped forward, and cut a single button from the Sergeant Major's tunic. It tumbled like a leaf to the ground. A challenge, a wera. Like, Matua thought, when a warrior greeted manuhiri at the marae. But that was just protocol, playacting, a prelude to friendship. This was a different thing entirely. He could see what the lieutenant was doing. He didn't quite have enough justification to attack Sergeant Major Blunt. So instead he was trying to make him snap. Like along the border, the British were constantly trying to needle the Māori into attacking, so that they would have an excuse to fight back.

But Sergeant Major Blunt was wise enough to see the strategy too, and did not respond.

Matua remembered the uneasy silence that fell when a visiting messenger from a hostile or uncertain tribe presented themselves unexpectedly at his father's kainga, seeking to informally sound out the possibility of cutting a deal or making a formal alliance. It was not quite the formal welcome of the marae, but nor was it the easy handshake of the British. Something different, somewhere between distrust and mutual need. Never trust a wardeal completely, his father had taught him, no matter how eagerly the burnt cloak changes hands   and how many speeches are made on the marae, or toasts drunk at the great pre-battle feast. Times change, needs change, these deals are only ever formed for a season. Often a chief will come to ask for your help in dispatching a rival, already planning to turn on you when you are weakened by fighting his war. That was how this conversation was now, he thought, as if the lieutenant was trying to work out how much he needed the Sergeant Major and whether it was worth fighting him now or later. Thomas thought it was like watching the beginning of a hunt, when the Master Of Hounds would let away a fox on purpose, only for the fun of chasing it to death slowly later.

A bugle blew. The men began to scatter. Sergeant Blunt stepped backwards, away from the bayonet. "Come on boys. That's Retreat they're playing, which means we need to settle you down for the night. Bring your tins, you can finish eating in the tent."

He kicked away the button into the mud. "Not a problem at all sir. Don't trouble yourself about it. There's plenty more where that came from in the stores. Get myself a new jacket where you accidentally snipped at it, too. Better be careful with that bayonet, though. Waving it around like that, you might do yourself a mischief. Only speaking out of concern for your own safety. Sir."

The men around them giggled. Blood rose in the lieutenant's cheeks. Then it was replaced by a disdainful, bored expression. Watching him, Matua felt it wasn't quite sincere: he was pretending not to care, but actually he was furious.

"I suppose next you'll want to tuck them up and read them a bedtime story from one of your foreign books. I suggest you try the tale of the Fox and the Crow in Lafontaine. But be warned, take heed. The Crow begins with all the food, but is not as clever as he thinks."

Languidly, he strolled away towards the noise and laughter of the beer tents outside the camp. Then, as if unable to resist the temptation of a final jab, he turned and yelled over his shoulder.

"Do what you like. But don't get too fond of them. From what I can gather, the little native prince will likely be dead in a few days."

River Time
The End of the Anthropocene

Down south lived Te Whete-a-Muturangi. the great octopus. Kupe met him, so they say, or so they say they say, or so they say they used to say but now they say no more, and they fled further down in each other's dark embrace to where the battle to the death began. Kupe won, of course. Such a clever boy. Hape would not have stood a chance. Better that the turtle treated him gently. Carried him over the surface of the sea.

But even Kupe couldn't win against my current. Waikato, the current of water, that is what my name signifies and you can feel its sharp pull even far out into the sea. No one defies my current and lives. I am not cruel by nature, but I am harsh and strong. You cannot separate a river from its current, any more than you can take people's longing for their land, or uplift a mother's love from her son.

Waikato taniwha rau, te piko he taniwha. It is true, the old saying. I am the Waikato of a hundred taniwha, there is a taniwha at every bend. But, at the end of the day, which is also a geological era, and at the end of the infinity of human time, which is also only a moment in the universal sight, the sight of the universe beholding itself, you might say, just as the river beholds its own reflection and is pulled along by its current towards its inevitable ending, the chaos and entropy of the sea. Ah, but the taniwha, I hear you say, waving your books and old stories. The taniwha is different. Why, that proverb does not just refer to the old creatures but also to the great chiefs. Waikato was known for the quality of its leadership, why -

What was I saying? A river can meander. Ah yes, at the end of it all, what is a taniwha? The horse eels dance in the boglands of Connemara, and the Shannon river has its peistes that taunt fisherfolk and refuse gleefully to be caught in mortal nets. Now the wetlands of the Waikato run beside the river like a new coat on a European boy's back. Or they do, in some times, but in others they have been drained and turned into farming dumps, where sheep and cows' piss replaces my soft waters. No native wetland fish can survive in this.

A soft catastrophe. A massacre of the species, taking place in plain sight. "A single death is a tragedy: a million deaths is a statistic." An ugly man, your Stalin, but he knew his brutish human psychology. History, they say, is told by the winners. When you have killed all the fish and each other, when every inch of soil lies bare and only the rocks and rivers are left, who will tell that tale?

Only me. Only me, whispering into the empty sea.

2019

Great South Road, Otatahu

He was a middleaged man, paunchy. He greeted them at the door with beer on his breath. He must have been expecting them, but already in his dressing gown. As he opened his mouth to say hello, Adele saw the yellow rat-like teeth she remembered from endless awkward Skype calls.

"Adele Wairere Smith. You're her father? ID? If you can just sign here, sir." Delivering me like a parcel, Adele thought. As if I'm not a person at all.

He took a pen in unsteady hands, and signed where they pointed. Then he gave Adele a big, sloshy, unaffectionate kiss. As if he wanted to show her that he could, rather than that he wanted to make her welcome. His lips pressed hard on his cheek.

"Well, haven't you grown," he sneered.

The police officers unlocked Adele's hands awkwardly, not looking at her as she did so. "We'll leave you to take it from here," Acne nodded. "She hasn't eaten. We offered her a Mcdonalds, but apparently that kind of thing is beneath her. Not above trying to give us a knuckle sandwich, though. Most unladylike."

All three men laughed.

Her father – it was hard to think of him as that, because he hadn't been around for so long, he was just the horrible man who made her talk to him on Skype, and occasionally made her mother cry - took them to the door, thanking them profusely for their time.

Then he turned around, and looked Adele up and down.

"Well, that was a lot of money I wasted on lawyers trying to get you here. You look like your mother. Ugly and dumb."

Adele was too shocked to speak. He saw her frozen face, laughed, went to the fridge

and took out a couple of beers. "Do you want one?" She shook her head.

"I'm underage. If you didn't know that."

"Of course I know that, that's why you're here. Sure you don't want a drink? It's legal, at home, if your parent offers it to you. And I am your father, whether you like it or not. Might make you a little less uptight." She shook her head.

He laughed. "Suit yourself."

She stood, awkwardly, looking around the room. "Where do I sleep?"

"On the couch for now. I only rented this place a few days ago. We'll get you a bed and the rest when I can see you've settled into school nicely." He laughed. "Stick and carrot, just like the old days. None of this modern touchy feely home education lark. You bring home good reports, you get a bed and mattress of your own. You don't do well at school, you'll get a belting."

"You can't hit children nowadays. That's the law."

"Sure it is. That's why I know how to do it without leaving any marks."

"But why?" Adele demanded, despairingly. "Why do this to us now?"

He turned on the TV without answering.

She looked around the room. He had obviously only just moved in. A few possessions, clearly bought from the cheapest stock at the Warehouse. Empty beer bottles, lining the window sill. Mould everywhere. Very Auckland. Her mother and she wiped the windows down every morning and used bleach to keep the ceiling spot-free, but clearly no one here had bothered for months. Asthma would be a problem here, she could see that now.

"Can I have something to eat?"

He didn't turn round. "You were offered food earlier and you said no."

Adele tried to sound apologetic. "I wasn't hungry then."

"Hard cheese. I've got no money myself at the moment. It's not cheap getting an emergency application into court – of course I'll make it all back and then some, now I won't be paying that bitch child support."

"Is that what this is about? You got that big job and you didn't want the child sup-

port bill?" Adele had promised herself that when she arrived she would give her father a fair chance and not jump to conclusions, but now she was too angry to care.

He shrugged. "Do you really think fathers do this because they want their screaming bratty kids?"

At that moment, the theme tune for On Demand Shortland Street started. Which was probably a blessing in the circumstances, Adele thought. A blessing. Now she was starting to sound like Ben and Rosemary. Still, there were clearly worse people to imitate. She desperately wished they were here.

After a while, she dozed off on the floor. Now he was slumped on the sofa. Adele wanted to go to bed, but there was nowhere to go. She shook him, gently.

"Um, dad? Can I -?"

He woke up with a start, and rubbed his eyes. "What the fuck, can't a man take a kip in his own –" Then he saw Adele, and lurched forward menacingly. "CYNTHIA? After all this time, you – didn't I give you enough of a hiding – "

"Dad, it's me. Adele. Your daughter. Cynthia's not here."

He grabbed her by the collar. "Don't you dare ever come near me again, don't you remember I said that? Or I'll fucking kill you. I'll kill you. Did you think I didn't mean it, you stupid cow?"

He started to put his hands over her mouth. His yellow teeth snapped wildly, as if he were a rat preparing to bite.

Calm, thought Adele. Try to keep calm. Remember how brave you were earlier. He doesn't know who you are, he's too drunk. Keep him talking. She jerked her head back, so that she could speak.

"School, daddy," she said in her best little girl voice, trying not to let her voice shake, "you need to let me go to bed now so I can be ready for school in the morning."

He looked at her with mad, confused eyes.

"They sent me to a school for bad boys and girls. I stole a loaf of bread. Not my fault, we were hungry. If you didn't work, you starved. That's how it was, back in those days. Not like now, all this social security and living on the benefit like you and your mother managed." He made a disgusted sound. "No, we had to work for our living. Hell on earth, it was. I would never have survived if that fella James hadn't taken me on – the things he made me do were disgusting, but at least he fed me – so don't try to make me feel sorry for you know, Cynthia, I could never make you suffer half as much as he did to me- "

"I'm not Cynthia. I'm your daughter," Adele said, desperately. "Look, dad, I love you." Shuddering at the necessity of it, she leant forward and kissed him on the cheek.

"Mum was afraid of you, wasn't she? That's why she ran away. But I'm not, see?"

He blinked, and rubbed his cheek, as if the kiss was an unknown, astonishing event. Adele held her breath. He looked her in the eye, confusedly. But not the mad confusion, the kind she'd seen before. This was a different kind of irrational, the waking up out of a dream kind, when you thought you knew where you were but you weren't quite sure yet.

Yes, reason had returned. He knew who she was again.

But it wasn't the kind of reason you wanted to see. He

was all awake now, all clearheaded. His eyes glittered like his ratty teeth in the streetlight that shone through the window. He was looking at her intelligently again, but with the knowing look a torturer might give his victim. It was a hot night, and they were sweaty from the struggle, but all of a sudden Adele felt very cold. "Your mother got away from me before I killed her," he breathed, without letting her go, "damned be those feminists and women's refuges. But never mind that, now I've got you."

Adele worked one hand behind her. The empty beer bottle. She grasped it in her hand and crashed it hard, down on the floor.

To her relief, it broke. The crash startled them both, even Adele. Her father's hand slackened on her arm.

She whirled away. To her feet. The arm, which did not seem to be hers any more, pointing the jagged broken bottle at him. A harsh, rasping voice, that she did not know. "Let me go, or I'll slash you. I'll do it, I swear. I'm a bad person, just like Mum."

He cowered. Swore at her. She backed to the door.

Then out on the road, running.

After a while, she stopped, and was sick. Vomiting up her father, and the broken bottle, and what she'd said. Perhaps she was a violent type at all. Perhaps she'd inherited it from him.

1862

Pokeno

On the move, again. Thomas tried to count the number of times he had been moved around since being kidnapped, as he now realised was what the Reverend Simpson and Mr James had done. Was it only a week ago? It felt like ten.

The telegraph turned out to be a sort of abbreviated letter, the kind that he and Matua used to scrawl on their slates at the back of the classroom. It was sent not by messenger boy but along a wire. Sergeant Major Blunt took them to see how it was tapped out. The birdwires disappeared downwards into a tent and ended in a machine that tapped the table in front of them like a very feeble hammer. A sandy-haired sapper crouched before a table, taking dictation from the contraption that whirred out dots and dashes at the speed of the bullets used in target practice outside.

"Morse code, lads. It's the future. You should learn it. The more you know about technology, the better your life chances will be. And this new way of sending messages is the business. Why, I hear they're even laying cable across the Atlantic now."

The message, when it came, was not too unwelcome. BOTH BOYS AWARDED SCHOLARSHIP AT SCHOOL IN PANMURE STOP SEND UNDER ARMED GUARD STOP INFORM BOTH FAMILIES OF THEIR SAFETY STOP TREAT WELL.

Which was all fine, except the request that they be treated

well. Because surely the British Army were supposed to do nothing else? And why couldn't they go home?

"You're hostages," Blunt explained when he asked him. They were sitting in their tent and he had brought brought the scored paper across to show them. "I don't like it much, but that's the way it is."

Matua chewed his lip. It made sense. "The Governor wants me living in Auckland to ensure that my father doesn't rise up against the British."

It was a nuisance, but it could have been worse. Sometimes rival tribes kept the peace in similar ways, by sending their sons to be educated or even their daughters married. A nicer word for it was diplomatic alliance. It was what it was. You didn't have to like it, but it came with the responsibility of being the son of a chief.

Most importantly, he would be safe. He knew perfectly well that his father had no intention of stirring up trouble. If war broke out, he had already indicated that he would remain neutral unless his own grounds were attacked. The Lieutenant must have been trying to scare them, that night when they first arrived. This was chess, not draughts, where you tried to destroy everyone. Chess had different pieces and different rules. Here he was just a pawn, to be moved around where convenient. No one wanted to kill him at all. Not like the game of trying to capture the King.

It was ironic, though. Thomas didn't know how much trouble their friendship had already caused him. During wrestling training at the whare wananga, the older boys had picked him out for the toughest fights. At first he had thought it was a compliment, but gradually he had realised that he was being punished. Was it for his father, who wanted to avoid the curse of trading with Europeans and keep to traditional Māori ways? Or was it himself, for going to whiteboy school and learning the language of the invader? He could not be sure, but the bruises were real. Often, after fights, he was left to eat his lunch alone, as

if the others wanted to emphasise that he was cut off by
the choices he had made. He wondered how he would be
treated when he came home again, and if any of the other
Māori wananga students would ever understand that this
whole situation was not his choice.

He must have looked gloomy, because Serjeant Major
Blunt squatted down beside him.

"You can take comfort, I suppose, in the fact that your
predicament is a very common one. We are all prisoners of
a kind. Man is born free, but is everywhere in chains."

Thomas thought of Father Murphy, with his endless
lectures about sin. They seemed harsh and unforgiving,
which was strange for such a lovable man. "Do you mean,
we are chained to our sinful desires and can only find
freedom in the love of Christ Almighty?"

Blunt shook his head. "No. That's exactly the opposite of
what I mean. The world is changing – there are new ways of
seeing these things – boys, I don't want to take away your
faith, if it helps you find comfort at a difficult time. But
remember this. Religion doesn't have to be the answer, if
you don't want it to be." He hesitated. "I'll be honest with
you, since you've been such good lads for me. Don't shout
it round the camp, or the padre will get upset. But speaking
for myself. I've no time for this idea of a Creator at all."

Both Matua and Thomas gasped. Why, Thomas had his
saints and Matua his nature gods. Different peoples, they
could see, spoke the hidden truths of faith in different ways.
But both were in natural agreement that behind them was
SOMETHING unified, holy and real. Otherwise it would
all be a sham, the kneeling for the Holy Sacrament and the
karakia before going to fish. They both knew to fast before
tapu activity, whether that was church or marae or hunting.
These were the ways you kept yourself aligned with the
holy order of the universe. Ponu, Faith, was important. It
was how you chose the right mana, power, to be dominated
by. If you didn't keep close to the right spirits the wrong

spirits would come and possess you. The only kind of person who didn't worship gods must, they both felt, be a sort of demon.

But here was Sergeant Major Blunt, with his twinkling eyes, and his daily box of biscuits and cake to keep them going between plentiful meals. Thomas had always thought people were only kind because they were frightened of going to hell if they didn't do good to others, but now he could see that was not quite true. Blunt did good because it was right. Perhaps that was better for the world, in the end. He was definitely not a demon, at any rate.

Demons, they both knew, brought sickness and harm. But Blunt wanted them healthy. He had sent the doctor to see Thomas, since he had had such a bad knock on the head. There was a great lump now, and the headaches kept coming and going. Sometimes he fell over unexpectedly, not quite fainting but dizziness.

"We call it concussion," the camp doctor told him. "Or shaking of the brain. The best treatment is rest, and it doesn't look like you've had much of that for a bit. So stay in bed while you're here, and I'll make sure you're transferred to Auckland by horse and cart."

Matua was in better shape, but the doctor still took a look at him. "You've been battered and bruised a bit, I want you to watch those cuts so that they don't get infected. Are you brave? I've heard Māori boys are. Good. Then you need to wash each wound with salt water twice a day. It will sting like hell, but you need to do it. And keep the wounds bandaged, and keep yourself clean."

Matua looked at him with interest. This was exactly the kind of knowledge his people needed. If he had to be educated by the British, he might as well take the chance to learn all about their warfare methods. "Why salt? I know our people who live close to the sea do that after a battle, but why is it?"

The young camp doctor was not busy that day. He talked

to them about how salt prevented infection. No one knew why, but it did. Sometimes you could save a leg or arm by applying salt early enough. He had learnt that from his brother, who was in the Navy. Hard to get theArmy to adopt new treatment like that, but it was happening slowly. He told them the new ideas of wound care and hygiene that were coming out of the terrible mistakes that had been made in the Crimean War. Florence Nightingale has been there and her methods were gradually being accepted. Only a woman, of course, but she'd nonetheless had some good ideas.

He showed them both how to roll a bandage properly, and apply it to a bleeding wound so that there was a chance of saving the limb, as well as stopping blood. Then he insisted that they both be brought clean clothes.

The cart arrived the next morning. To Thomas' relief, it had been filled with hay. They clambered up and took their places. Blunt was there to see them off, and insisted that their hands were not tied. "We've been told to treat them well. They've been awarded a scholarship, for heaven's sake. Can't deliver them to receive their prize in chains."

Thomas lay down on the back, and Matua sat beside him. Two guards with pistols and sabres rode front and back. Matua knew they were guards, and he was a prisoner, but to others it must look like a royal escort. I'm being treated like a prince, he thought ruefully. Might as well enjoy it whilst it lasts.

"Now lookee, lads." Blunt came over and rearranged Thomas' blanket. "Take my advice and treat it as an adventure. There's never any harm in education, and who knows you might pick up some new skills and ideas, or even better find some good friends at this place."

He laughed. "I'm a Quartermaster and I tell you, what Napoleon said about an army marching on its stomach is wrong. Soldiers march for each other and fight for each other. Not for Queen and country, but for friends.

Friendship can make the worst siege bearable, so make sure you two stick together and stick up for each other." The guards nodded approvingly. "Now a word as to your futures. I expect they'll teach you Greek and Latin, which I never got. But one day you'll leave and need to earn an honest living.

Thomas, if you ever want to enlist then make sure it's to my regiment and I'll keep an eye on you. But my advice is, to you both, learn what you can in Auckland and when you've finished your education, get right back to farming. Grow your own food and keep out of the way of war."

He pursed his lips, as if trying to make a decision. His hands fiddled with the blanket. Now they were trembling. He lowered his voice.

"And if you get a chance, escape. I don't like this setup at all. I'd have helped you to get away myself if you were stronger. Keep your wits about you and get back home as soon as you possibly can."

2019

Great South Road

The river runs like a road. So when Kupe came in his canoe across the Waitemata gulf, there were so many fish, he feared that he could not cleave a way through them with his craft. And now there are so few, all the food is tins and packages, and people are growing hungry in the cities. That night Adele slept in a shop doorway, covering her face with her hood so no one could see she was a young girl. In the morning she walked down the road with no money in her pocket and no idea of where to go. A taxi passed, and slowed for her hopefully. She nodded and climbed in.

"Where to?" Adele didn't know Auckland so she said the only place she had heard of, which is Great South Road. "But we're on that already," said the taxi driver, "Do you mean south or north?"

"South," she shrugged, and they drove for a few minutes in silence until the taxi driver, working on a growing suspicion born of sharp observation and experience, asked her if she had money for a fare.

"No."

"How old are you?"

"Too young to have money of my own."

He scratched his turban thoughtfully. "I see," he said, in his Punjabi accent, which was still strong despite having lived in Auckland for thirteen years, "and if you have no money to pay me do you have any money for food?"

She shook her head. This is Taamaki,where the old

Māori proverb says "Taamaki:
kainga nga ika me nga wheua katoa!" Taamaki, where you can eat fish, bones and all! And now she and so many like her are hungry. He drove on for another few minutes, and turned off Great South Road to where the Takanini gurdwara shines high and joyful amongst the dismal rotting state houses. "Go in there."

"Why? I'm not religious."

"Go in there. Wash your hands, take your shoes off and cover your head. You can come every day if you want to. They'll let you eat for free."

She did as she was told, as best she could. Shoes off was straightforward enough:

made sense, like being on the marae with Granma, and anyway there were shelves clearly set aside for the purpose. Women's and men's shoes, laid out in neat rows. Like a secondhand shop, except that these were not for sale.

Harder was covering her head. She had her hoodie on, of course, but she was pretty sure that was not the taxi driver meant. A deep box of scarves, next to the public sinks. But how to make them stay on her head? There were small orange ones, that looked more like kerchiefs. She tried one on for size, but it didn't feel quite right. A longer, swishier one, but slightly seethrough. She could wrap it around her head and neck like a hijab, but would its chiffon fabric be modest enough? Well, it must be, she reasoned, they had left it out for visitors to use.

She washed her hands as she'd been told, and followed the crowd into the dining hall. Pictures, that she supposed were of Sikh saints. Some of them were fighting, was that against the British or other Indians? How strange to think that the ancestors of the people here, or the sacred ancestors on the walls, might have fought against some of the very soldiers who'd then been shipped over here to build the road outside.

Now food was here. Thank the heavens. Roti bread and

curry, some sweet rice dish. Pickles and yoghurt. And tea, thank goodness, sweet milky tea. She was suddenly too shaky to hold the tray they had given her, and almost let it drop. A woman held her up: then staggered with Adele's weight. She hadn't fainted, quite, but she was too dizzy to stand. The same young man who had brought her in rushed to assist, and together they guided her to one of the seats by the wall. These, she could see, were reserved for the very elderly: everyone else sat on the floor. Elderly and infirm, she thought ruefully, that is me today.

She ate, and sat still, until she began to feel a little better. A young girl came up with a basket of roti. "More?" she asked, in English. Adele shook her head. The woman who had helped her to the seat stopped by, on her way out. "Feeling better?" Adele nodded. After that she was left alone, not in the annoying cliquey way she had experienced at some homeschool social groups, but with a sort of respectful discretion, as if no one wanted to embarrass her by asking why she had come for food. The young man in the orange scarf waved at her as he left, then ducked down on his knees to kiss his hands, which he then touched reverently to the floor. Like that genuflection thing Cynthia is always complaining about, thought Adele. She thought it was disgusting, making you kneel to the priests. It didn't seem wrong here, though. Nothing to do with worship, really. Just being grateful for the fact you'd had some food.

There was a word that came onto her lips, when she thought about it. Thankyou. Not to a god, or to an idea of how the world was made, or to a holy book. She didn't feel she could ever go with any of that nonsense, it wasn't how she had been raised and it would never suit her, it just didn't feel anything like home. But here, in the gurdwara, she did want to thank something or someone, for the fact that she'd found somewhere to eat today.

An image rose in her mind, of the great Waikato river. One holiday years back Cynthia had taken her to the Huka

Falls. They had arrived in the evening, when the waters ran like an angry blue ribbon through the dusk. It was odd to be in a moment that was both so violent, and so tender. The waters were wild, untamable, frightening. You would be pulverised in a second if you stepped into them, yet here they were, watching safely from the bank.

And the river was like a guardian, wasn't it? That was what all the old stories of taniwha meant. Lots of cultures had their stories of river monsters. Cynthia and she had even done a project together on it. But the different peoples treated the boundary between nature and supernatural in different ways. You could think of the as if it lived in the river, like the Irish did, or you could see it as the river itself, a sort of spirit, above and beyond and within. That was the Māori way, no real differentiation. The Waikato was a taniwha itself. A good taniwha, the kind that fed and watered and provided for people. Even up here in Auckland, she was pretty sure, the water that ran in the taps and bathrooms came from the Waikato. And she knew you must treat a taniwha with respect.

Gratitude, even.

"Thank you," she said to the river, and felt, for now, at home.

2019

Hamilton

In hospital, every day was the same. First they came in with their blood pressure machines and checked that he hadn't died overnight. He hadn't, of course, although they had nearly driven him mad by waking him several times to make sure. He'd broken into pieces a few times, of course. Fallen off the bed in black juddering moments when his eyes watered splinters of light and the world around him broke into tiny mosaic pieces, squiggly lines.

He'd known it wasn't demons. He'd known that for a while, no matter how many times his parents and the pastor prayed. He knew the world was billions of years old and he doubted the rest of the Bible too. He wouldn't have admitted it, though, not even to Adele. But his body didn't care about upsetting people. His body jerked and frothed and turned into .

They wanted to start him on anti-epileptic medication, but his mother was refusing. She wanted to try prayer for a bit longer, she said. After all, the demons had always eventually given up and gone away before. The doctors held long meetings with her, and even longer ones on their own. A social worker turned up and asked him questions. He turned his face to the wall and waited until she gave up and went away. She seemed nice enough, but after what had happened to Adele he wasn't fool enough to open his mouth when she was there.

The nights were easier, because his mother wasn't allowed

in the ward and everyone else left him alone. Morning was signalled not by daylight – he was in a windowless room – but by the rattle of the teatray, and the change over from night staff. First they did the handover, then they brought around breakfast.

This was OK, except that by the time the toast made its slow way up to the ward, it was cold. It didn't matter much because Ben wasn't very hungry, which was odd because he couldn't remember a time when he wasn't ravenous.

Apart from the meds, Rosemary brought him everything he asked for and a lot he didn't, trying to tempt his appetite. Even Mcdonalds, which were usually vetoed. He did his best to try to please her, but he couldn't manage more than a few mouthfuls.

He wasn't a prisoner, exactly. No one had locked the door. But he was in a private room with glass windows. Like being in a goldfish bowl, only even a goldfish could swim around, and he couldn't get out of bed. His legs shook and he had to be wheeled to the toilet on a commode. He was in an adult ward, because the children's ward was full, due to a measles epidemic which was probably the result of the anti-vaxxers who were flooding homeschool websites with their propaganda about how vaccines are causing everything from global warming to autism. He hoped there'd never be a pandemic in his lifetime, because clearly if so everyone he knew through homeschool and church would probably refuse to take a vaccine and be wiped out. Which might be a good demonstration of the process of natural selection, but also might be, you know, catastrophic. To lose everyone you knew, overnight. Horrific. That must be Adele right now. He wondered where she was, and if they'd ever see each other again.

The private room was for his own safety, because the paediatricians thought he needed to be under close supervision. Because of the selfharming, which was obviously a problem, especially as he couldn't explain it.

Which meant that, effectively, he was being locked up for his own safety. His bags had been confiscated "just in case." Which, he supposed, meant just in case he was hiding a knife in there with which to damage himself again. Even Rosemary wasn't allowed to bring anything in to give to him unless it was checked. He had wifi, on his phone, but his head and eyes hurt from the seizures so it was hard to watch anything for long.

Rosemary wanted to have him out of the hospital as quickly as possible. It was a heathen place, she scoffed, Satan's influence was in play although she admitted that the staff seemed kind. But you couldn't trust them or their medicines. What if they only cured the physical symptoms, but not the underlying cause? Ben'd be running around with a demon in him. Evil, inside and out, eating him away. No, she wouldn't let the hospital do more than monitor him. He'd go home with her and the prayer cell group would come and lay hands. Anoint him. She even offered to bring him back to the hospital. But the doctors weren't about to agree, and now that Oranga Tamariki was sniffing around the situation, even Rosemary could see that she was inviting trouble if she discharged him herself. So she'd gone back to Auckland on her own to pray with the pastor.

Ben missed her, of course, but it was a lot quieter without the Hallelujahs and constant praying in tongues.

"Hi, Ben." A voice at the door. Too early for visiting time.

"It's Sheila and Mark, they said we could come in this morning and say hi since your mum can't come in today. As long as we don't stay long."

It was so good to hear a familiar voice.

"Hey, Ben." Mark was clearly doing his absolute best to be restrained. "How is it life in hospital?"

"Great, Mark," Ben said, trying to sit up. "They're really nice here. You'll love it when it's your turn."

Sheila shot him a grateful look. He knew that Mark had a tonsil operation coming up.

"Your mum has had to go up to Auckland. She'll be back tonight." She produced a large bar of chocolate. "Here, I know it's not the healthiest, but –"

Ben tried to look grateful. "Thanks so much." He wanted to ask how Adele was, but realised that no one who had any contact with Cynthia would be allowed to know.

Mark noticed the commode by his bed. Fortunately it was clean. "Can I play on that?"

"Oh no, Mark –" Sheila began to say, but he was out of the door and scooting along the corridor. "Ben needs that!" she called after him with little effect.

"Don't worry." Ben shrugged. "I used it just a few minutes ago."

At that moment, the shakes began. Limbs spread-eagled over the bed, like a giant hyperactive spider. The episode lasted for a minute or so, then stopped abruptly. His head rolled sideways. He was used to it by now, he knew how to zone out and stop panicking, but it was a new experience to see the horror on Sheila's face.

"Shall I call the nurse?"

"No need. It happens a lot. They want to start me on epilepsy meds – but we have to wait till Mum and Dad speak to the pastor, come back - "

"Oh, for goodness sake. They're not refusing?"

"Still deciding. They wanted time to think. She'll be back tonight."

Down the Great South Road, he caught himself thinking, absurdly. Riding down on his horse to invade. But that was ridiculous. The Great South Road still existed, but it petered out at the Bombay Hills. Anyone coming to Hamilton would use Highway One. The one that cut through the remains of Rangiriri Pa. Where something very important had happened, he remembered Sheila telling them a few days ago as they had driven past, but he couldn't remember precisely what.

"Well, I hope they show some common sense soon.

Anyway." Sheila gathered herself together, placing her worry about Ben's health somewhere appropriately distant, like Mark crashing up and down in the corridor. "I brought you some clothes."

"Thanks, but I'm not allowed them. They want me in a hospital gown in case I try to escape." He showed her his red tag, ruefully.

"If you've brought boxer shorts, I can have those. They give you this awful disposable hospital underwear –"

He remembered the woman nurse telling him he could keep his own underwear on, and the pathetic sense of gratitude he had felt. You lost so much in hospital, he thought. You had to be grateful for every small thing you could hang onto, even your underwear and your name. That was what Oranga Tamariki didn't understand. On her last visit, the social worker had asked him if he was happy at home. What a stupid question, Ben thought. It wasn't a question of being happy or unhappy. Home was who you were. You couldn't be yourself, properly, anywhere else.

"Sure." Sheila rummaged in the bag she had brought. "They're here. I'll put them in that cupboard."

She bent over. Her lowcut top showed interesting curves, at least Ben thought he was supposed to find them interesting. The thought concerned him. He had used to think his lack of interest in women's figures was a moral thing, that he'd just learnt enough about Biblical sins of the flesh to be particularly good at resisting the temptations of lust. He was starting to realise that there was more to it than that. No matter how he tried to wank over women, it was images of boys that kept coming into his head.

The thought of girls reminded him of Adele. "How's Cynthia doing?"

"She's a total mess."

"And Adele? Any news? Do we know where she is now?"

Sheila looked suddenly shifty. "I've no idea. Why would I be told?" She finished unpacking the clothes with a sudden burst of speed. "There. Done. Now, I don't know if you want them, but Mark has finished with these magazines, I know they're probably a bit childish..."

Ben took them politely. *The Beano.* He would send them down to the children's ward after she had left.

"And, since your mother's not here, I thought you should have this." She pulled out a battered white cardboard box. "I mean, just because you're in hospital is no excuse for getting behind on your history project." She was joking, of course. At least Ben hoped she was.

The unwelcome sound of the social worker's high heels clattered down the corridor. "Oh, sorry Ben, I see you've got company. I'll come back in half an hour." Her voice was a nasally grate. Sheila recognised the swinging lanyard and leapt up.

"Look, I just want to say, Ben's family are great people. And I'm sure they're going to make wise and sensible decisions. You don't have to - "

The social worker closed the door, without bothering to answer. Sheila banged her fist against the wall. "Shit."

Ben opened the lid. But there were only papers.

"Where's the - "

"The taiaha? I've put it somewhere safe."

"Not at the museum?"

"No. Actually, I've had another idea as to what we might do." Ben waited for her to say more, but she didn't expand.

"You know what Mark said about the man with a knife, at your church?"

Sheila looked at him oddly. "Yes?"

"Was that true? I mean, did it really happen?"

"Yes. Last year."

"Why wasn't it in the newpapers? I mean...." He fought for words. "You would think. That's an atrocity. In New Zealand..."

Sheila sighed. "We're Jews, Ben. We've survived in all sorts of places. No one died. No one hurt. Why court trouble? Kiwi Jews, our policy is to keep a low profile, not make trouble for anyone. Put up with the small shit, so the big shit doesn't happen. Do our best to keep out of harm's way."

Ben shook his head. "But that's wrong. You shouldn't have to."

"But we do. You ask Cynthia about Jews and the Family Court sometime." Sheila wouldn't say more.

It was afternoon by the time Ben felt well enough to look through the box. He wasn't wild about history, but it beat waiting for the next seizure.

Old, spidery writing. Photographs. Names on the back, which he didn't recognise. He would have to ask his mum when she came back, see if she knew who they were. Pity Gran was dead, she had known more about the family history than them.

A letter caught his eye. It was written in careful copperplate, almost too perfect, as if the writer did not have full confidence in his own handwriting.

"On the instructions of my superiors I have journeyed to the south in recent weeks, and I can say with absolute confidence that the rumours that are sweeping Auckland of an imminent Māori invasion are simply not true. The Māori is passionate about self-improvement and education. Why, at this very moment there are five hundred Māori boys in boarding schools across the Waikato district.

Moreover, the standard of education is clearly high, my inspections show that the Māori child is quite as capable as arithmetic as the European. My conclusions are that the Māori seeks European education and opportunities for commerce, not war. I would urge my superiors to ask Grey to reconsider this dangerous plan to disturb a prosperous and settled people who wish nothing more than to live in peaceful alliance with Her Majesty. Let us build this road, if we must, but let it be to bring greater trust and commerce between the peoples. Let it not be a road to war."

The letter was dated January 1862 and signed, Sergeant Blunt.

He put it back into the box, and took out another. This was thicker and darker ink. Almost bloodlike, Ben thought. The writing scrawled in confident swirls across the page.

This made it harder to read.

"I have interrogated several of the ringleaders in the plot to sack Auckland that was hatched last year. It is quite clear that it was not a serious attempt, and simply idle talk from a few southern hotheads. The majority of the Waikato chiefs, and the King himself, opposed it. It came to nothing, and was abandoned even by the conspirators, once it was heard that Grey was coming back. The Maori leadership falsely believed that he would be more sympathetic to them than Gore Brown, and war was consequently regarded as unnecessary. I believe they were telling the truth."

The next sentence was underlined.

"<u>Sadly these warriors were utterly obdurate and could not be tempted into false confession</u> of current plans to attack Auckland, even under torture. I have noticed before that natives from the northern Waikato are remarkably hard to 'break.' My conclusion, therefore, is that unfortunately if we are to use native voices to persuade the citizens of Auckland and Great Britain that the Pakeha inhabitants of New Zealand are under imminent threat of attack, we may need to find a more childish songbird, to sing the type of song we need."

The letter was signed, simply, James.

Ben picked up another letter. This one was delicately written. The ink was so faded it was hard to read.

"Dear Mr James,

Thank you for your letter enquiring about my son Mark. He is doing well and I believe has learnt his lesson. There is no need for more investigation or concern. I must ask you to forgive me for my uncooperative demeanour, when you called to speak to me about my son's behaviour. I believe that he is a well-intentioned boy who is simply spirited, and there is no need to take drastic measures by sending him to the Reformatory. I assure you that whilst he is being brought up in the Jewish faith for now, there will be plenty of opportunity for him to acquaint himself with the Christian doctrine as an adult, if he so desires. I assure you, too, that no offence was intended to the young ladies in question and that far from wishing to indecently expose himself, my son was simply attempting to demonstrate an obscure aspect of one of our Talmudic passages, relating to the physical signs of maturity at which a young boy may be viewed as a man.

I do however understand that you are eager to find young people who would ben-

efit from the institutional care and humane reform approach that you are pioneering in Auckland. Further to this, may I respectfully suggest a home which is in an alarming state of untidiness..."

At that point the ink faded out, and the rest of the letter was illegible.

At the bottom of the box was a picture. An old schoolhouse, like the one he had seen at MOTAT. Rows of polite white pinafores, doffed caps, and in the middle, a frowning schoolteacher. Somewhere by the sea or a river, there was a stretch of water yawning empty behind them.

He looked again at the photograph. It made no sense. The picture clearly dated from the middle of the last century. The date was written in the corner. January 1862. But the stern schoolmaster. Thin lips, and pebbly eyes. Unmistakable. Which meant –

Ben lay back on the pillow, stretched his aching neck and thought. As he did so, the social worker popped her spiky blonde hair around the door again to ask if now was a good time to have a chat. This time, Ben told her to fuck right off.

1862

Great South Road

Panmure

Thomas lay on his back on the cart, looking up at the blue Auckland sky. The road followed the path of the telegraph poles, and he could see the familiar sparrows of home crowding it. Now he knew what the wires were really for, he wondered why the birds wanted them. Perhaps, having been detached from their homeland, they were confused and homesick and didn't fancy setting their feet on these funny foreign trees.

He liked sparrows, but it seemed strange that there were so many of them here. No native birds along this road now, whereas when he had come this way with his father and mother that sad journey southwards after burying his younger brother, he had managed to distract them from their silent grief with an excited shout at a new bird every hundred yards or so, followed by an animated discussion of what it might be called. That was only five years ago. Now the sparrows were here, they had driven every other bird away. The country was changing, fast, and you could see it happen, even in such a short time. Like the Fencible village of Onehunga, which had been so comfortingly ramshackle a few years ago. Now when they passed it distant on the horizon it looked unsettlingly neat and tidy to the sight, like a British country house garden. Probably a good thing that they hadn't gone there for help. It looked like attitudes might have changed.

They were travelling briskly, Matua noticed, but not anything like as briskly as the carts carrying fruit and other produce from the Māori farms south. He knew why the couriers were working at such speed. Ten years ago, they had had in Auckland a captive market. It was generally acknowledged that the Māori farming communities' skill and adaptability with argriculture was the only reason Auckland City was able to survive at all. They had moved with ease from a subsistence to a settled agricultural economy and were exceptional, it was generally agreed, at both the new European-style farming and trading the results.

Matua remembered travelling with his father as a young boy through the district. It was as if the world they knew had been lost to trade. Everywhere they went they were greeted not with enquiries about the health of their whanau and iwi but the price of wheat, pork and flax. Old kaumaatua did not discuss history and mythology around the fires any more, but the appearance and health of their crops. They had been startled, even more so when they found the women were occupied not in traditional handicrafts but in the making of baskets and legropes to carry grain and pigs to market. His father had been uncertain of the wisdom of this new approach, he recalled. He'd argued with the other chiefs about it.

"Hei kai kei aku ringa," they protested. Look, we are creating success by our hard work. There is food at the end of our hands.

His father had shaken his head, and thrown a proverb in return. "Ma whero ma pango ka oti ai te mahi." There are traditional ways of living, and they require being in cooperation with one another. If everyone does their part and works together, the work will be complete, like the black and red patterns on the walls of the meeting house. But this requires fellowship and working together, he said, not competing with other Māori to sell your wares to Auckland in the European way.

The chiefs of the new commerce had protested that they were industrious, and that Māori traditions valued hard work. "Moe atu nga ringa raupo," they insisted. Marry a man with calloused hands. Yes, Matua's father had agreed, hard work is important. But look not just at our traditions of hard work, but how we give and share. When we made too much for ourselves, we did not go into trading battle with each other like the Pakeha. Why, we made great feasts, the seadwelling tribes would bring thousands of dried fish and they would swap it for dried birds' meat from the forest tribes. This is a more productive way to live. Do not fall for this mess of coinage and argument over price. It is a slow death of the communal soul, this Pakeha business way. (That was why Matua had had to keep it a secret from his father, that he was selling fish to the soldiers on the road).

Prophets were popular amongst the Waikato tribes when they promised glorious visions of freedom, but not when they taught austerity and dull self-reliance. Eventually Matua's father had given up and gone home in despair. Then the crash had come, when in 1856 the market for wheat had crashed. The Māori had been left with rotting grain and embittered relations with their traders. Men had brawled in the streets of Auckland over the chance to sell their vegetables at a loss. It had improved now, somewhat, with the new markets for golddiggers in Otago, but never again would a Māori driver take for granted the urgent necessity of getting his produce to market in Auckland before someone else.

Now they were close to Auckland city. A bustle of houses and stores, many in wood and a few in stone. Matua could feel the awe stirring up in him. This is what the lads at wrestling practice didn't understand, there was a new world being built up here and you didn't have to hate all of it. What if the Māori could take advantage of the new technology, build their own cities? If there was Pakeha Auckland in the North, and a Māori City of the King in the south? One could dream, surely? Better than going to war.

There were even more travellers on the road now. Some looked curiously at him. Most did not. Was a Māori boy invisible here, unless he was selling produce or serving them in the inns? But strangely, he was not the only person who seemed invisible. Towards evening, they passed a young girl with red hair travelling in the opposite direction. She was dressed in strange long breeches, with a hood over her head. She walked fast without looking where she went, as if she was trying to get away, but had no idea where she was going. Beside her walked a man in a turban, like the pictures he'd seen of India during Empire geography lessons. He offered her food, and she accepted it. But when Matua looked again, they were gone, just like the nature spirits he thought he might have once seen when he was young.

He didn't have time to think about it for long though, because they were almost at their destination. The front escort stopped to ask for directions.

"Panmure Industrial School." Black railings and high gates. Goodness, like a prison, Matua thought. This wasn't how he had expected the kind of school that gave out scholarships to look.

Thomas gave a groan. "It's not a school. It's an orphanage. Scholarship my foot."

"Inside." The guards were now curt and clipped, as if they too realised the trick that had been played on them and resented the kindness they had shown on the way. Thomas and Matua took the bundles of clothes that they had been gifted by Sergeant-Major Blunt, and stepped inside the gates. They shut with a depressing clang.

"Welcome to the Christian Mission, boys." A buxom woman in a black large hat with ribbons on the side stood with a mirthless smile. "Let me show you to the infirmary."

"Only one of them is unwell, madam. The little Mick."

"Oh, we quarantine all our new arrivals for a fortnight. Keeps the lice and fleas under control. We give them work whilst they're on the ward, of course. The Christian Mission does not encourage idleness. From day one our young charges learn the value of labour and the importance of earning their keep. Some are sent to us as criminals. All of them need reform. We are so hopeful of our colleague Mr James' plans for a more severe and secluded reformatory. Which reminds me. You gentlemen should be given some recompense for your long journey. I expect you haven't eaten."

She clapped her hands and called "Girls!" White-pinafores came down the stairs, yawning. They went to the kitchen and returned with bread and cheese. They looked tired and shabby, but not too thin, Thomas noted with relief. Clearly the industrial school provided adequate food. Coming from a country in famine, you tended to be alert to small details like this. He doubted there would be much in the way of education, except in areas that made the institution money, like sewing for the girls and carpentry for the boys. But it looked like they would be fed enough to stay healthy, and there was plenty of time to do as the Sergeant had suggested and plot a discreet escape.

He was partly right. The school did not officially exist to punish students for being poor, and it was the benign policy of the establishment to ensure everybody ate well who earnt an honest living. On the wards Thomas, with his concussion, found that the introductory task of stitching mailsacks for the new New Zealand postal system was beyond him. He could only do a couple of sacks a day, to Matua's ten.

Thomas did not think that much could make him feel worse, but on the third and final day of his stay, he saw a familiar face in the street. For a moment he thought he might be hallucinating, but then steadied himself: the diet might be dull and unappetising, but they were not <u>that</u> hungry. Yes, he was right, it was Mr James. Not, heaven be thanked, in the school itself, but watching their window, steadily, from the street outside. And beside him was a young boy, with ratlike yellow teeth. He was listening attentively to Mr James and watching them carefully too.

2019

Hamilton

Ben wanted to wake up, but the dream was too strong. He'd been in it for a while, first trapped in a glacier crack and falling out of the iceberg with the beginning of the global spring. The world was covered with ice, it always had been. His mother's cold stare when he asked a dangerous question. Glassy frozen water, impossible to see or think. But now it was melting. Ice groans, when it breaks. He didn't know a world that was not icebound.

He didn't want to be anywhere else.

The iceberg splintered irrevocably into a thousand pieces. You couldn't go back, put the pieces together again. Faith was like that, it was fragile. That is why you had to protect it, cover it with a layer of icy ignorance, not let too much sunlight or warmth on the globe. Now the Great Change had happened, and the place where he didn't need to think for himself because God and his parents had all the answers was buried in a torrent of melted water, drowned and irrecoverable. There was nothing to do but swim, and hope for the best.

He'd been trying to kick his legs and keep afloat. Sometimes there seemed to be a turtle that bore him up. Other times he was alone, tossing and turning in a terrible current. Somewhere had been an a, he had been a voyager, setting out from a distant land, to discover another one. Was he on a sailing ship, or a waka? He wasn't sure. It felt more and more as if he was riding a turtle, but that could not possibly be true.

The sky above him groaned and turned into a butterfly. That was Adele, only she didn't last long, but turned into a chrysalis. Ben tried to rescue her, but he was trapped too in a shell of his own. He'd been a kingfisher, and also a moth, but now his adult bodies were disintegrating. All that was left of him was sludge and skeleton.

A glittering dangerous angel flew past him, with Sheila's face. "Yes, I did it," she fluted, playing on her harp. "The Ministry came to my house to ask about Mark's sexualised behaviour. I was afraid they'd take him away, so I dobbed Cynthia and Adele in." She flew a little further up a tree, and gabbled nonsense like a bird.

"They don't like Jews, the Ministry. They think we're secretive. Keep to ourselves. I offered to send Mark to Jewish school, but they said that still wasn't a normal childhood. Conspiracy schmiracy. They're not anti-Semitic, but the school has high walls and they said that it was like a prison. What was I to do? Anyway. What I said was true. She does have a messy house. And she did take drugs before she had kids. Lilith ran away from Adam, too." She blurred into the distance, and the dream was gone.

Now Ben was in full seizure, and the world was a giddy string of ribbons that danced spaghetti trails. His mind was spilling out of him like guts from a filleted fish. Gutteral sounds drifted out of a mouth that belonged to someone else. He was above his own body, floating in a cloud of pain. You came into this country on the Trade Winds, whispered the stars. You brought us what you wanted to share and took the rest.

The Sheila angel was back. It whispered truth and also falsehood, as if it were a betrayer of true life, and also a simple prophet. Religion is a mighty river, and we are all swept along in its path. Lies are all that we have, when the truth is swept away by time. You may as well forget your home and family, boy, they will never let you out of here alive.

Then there was a rainbow bridge that spattered gore between heaven and earth. You could clatter across it and see the universe swaying and dark, burning itself out to nothing like a candle that had been frittered away. A horse pranced, ready to ride you to victory over the atoms and quarks that trapped you here. But it came with a warning, spilt in sharp light on the winter sky. This was a one-way journey. Once there you could never go back. Ben wanted to go, but his body stayed on the bed.

Then he was back inside himself. Paralysed, but alive. He could hear himself moan, but he couldn't move or see.

Instinctively, he reached to climb out of bed, and hit the guardrails. Oh, that's right, he was in hospital. He couldn't walk. He wanted to call someone and ask them to turn on the light, but it felt ridiculous to ask for help for something so unimportant and childish as a nightmare. Then he remembered something else: he could just take off his eye mask. The ward was lit day and night. He did so, wincing at the strength of the light. But at least they were reminding him he was awake, not drifting along in a terrible riversea that snapped at and jolted him as if he were being eaten away by eels that had pierced the bottom of his boat. His legs were heavy, like a club foot that dragged behind the turtle on its way to the cold far South. And there were no windows in this ward, because the tribe had blocked them out to keep him from running away, following the rest of the adventurers to sea.

"Hape," he moaned aloud, without understanding what he had said.

2019

Mangere Bridge

I'll never be clean. Not after what he did. That's the problem, you see. Here all the fancy types are on about organic food. But I'm already poisoned all the way through. You can't fix the kind of dirt that was done to me.

It doesn't matter how much I clean the toilets, go and hose myself down in the shower afterwards. I'm still covered with shit, inside and out. Shit of the mental kind, the kind you can't clear with a laxative and a bogbrush.

I don't remember much. It's just blurry bits in my memory, kind of like the censored bits of nudie photography on instagram. I remember being locked in a cupboard once, because I wouldn't do what he said.

It was dark, the cupboard, dark and no windows. When I sat on the frontline listening to those stories about Hape, I heard the bit about the windows being blocked up and I sort of froze. Because it's not just that we have the same name, see? It's what happened to him and me, it's too close for comfort. Except no turtle ever turned up to save me and take me to a promised land.

He rode me like a turtle though, Thin Lips. I was the one gasping for breath, trodden down by the weight of a grown man on top of me, so I could hardly breathe. Octopus hands, too, everywhere all over me. Nightmare. Like being dragged down to the bottom of the ocean. Only Kupe did that because he was a hero. And me, I was only there because I was too weak and small and stupid to run away.

I used to think of the amber taiaha when it was happening. Wonder if that might have protected me, and where it was gone.

Course, the Hape in the story had a club foot. I kind of envy that, because everyone knew to look at him. My dirt's invisible. It's almost worse, when it's something no one else you can't see..

He was a boss, Hape. Didn't take any shit. You the way Hape kept his wife but told everyone else to get stuffed? Made them go further south to find land, because this place was his alone? I love that bit. I'd do the same.

If I ever met my mum again, yeah, I'd be like Hape. She abandoned me, I'd tell her to get lost. Bet she's sitting eating organic vegetables right now. Nice clean easy life she's got for herself. Once she'd thrown dirty old me away.

1862

Panmure Industrial School

Now I'm an old man I have the time to remember to feel sorry for that boy with the ratty yellow teeth. Time to forgive him? Well, I'm not sure I'd go that far. There's a Jewish fella lives next door. he goes crazy every September before their big fast trying to forgive everyone he's ever met. He'd probably manage it. I'm not that type.

But as young Thomas I knew as soon as he walked into the ward he was trouble and wanted him gone.

Even if Thomas had not spotted him out of the window with Mr James, the way he tried to ingratiate himself with them as he arrived would have given it away.

One way you can tell a bad friend, or a traitor, spy, is that they do not tell you what they want you to know about themselves, good or bad, but they spend all their time making nasty dismissive remarks about other people. Thomas was too young to notice, but Matua had learnt how to spot those who couldn't be trusted on the whare wananga and marae. politics and tactics held in the whare wananga and marae. It was the tribes you couldn't trust that tried to bring your warriors on board their battle wakas by being vicious and uncompromising in their attacks on everyone else.

And another clue was that he'd arrived suddenly to stay with them on the infirmary ward, just before the end of the fortnight's isolation. He claimed to be a new pupil, name of Alf, but it was quite clear from the familiar way Matron spoke to him that they knew each other well. On probing, he agreed he had a Māori name too, but didn't remember it because he'd been adopted by a Pakeha man and that was his family now. What was the name of his Pakeha father? He mumbled something like Mr Jones. Mr James? He shook his head hastily. No, no, definitely not. All very ominous. Thomas and Matua agreed in whispers that they would not discuss anything important in front of him.

On the fourteenth morning after their arrival at the Industrial School, Thomas was unexpectedly allowed to get out of his pyjamas and presented with his clothes.

"But I'm still dizzy," he said. "The army doctor said I should rest until that stopped."

Matron sniffed. "You're well enough to walk downstairs to chapel and join the other children."

That was true, he probably was. Thomas felt reassured at the thought. Chapel would be something familiar. He wasn't entirely sure that Jesus and Mary had been listening properly to his earnest nightly prayers for rescue, but perhaps they would listen better there, and if not there would be some hymns and the sacrament. Thomas found great comfort in that idea. The Body of Our Lord, Father Murphy always said, will give you a miraculous consolation no matter how tired or afraid or fearful you are. "Just its taste on your tongue, when you are in dire need, will be like a blessing in times of hardship and trial. In fact, my boys and girls," he had told the First Communion class, "I will go so far as to say that you will be able to judge the degree of danger and hardship in your worldly affairs by the depth of longing which you find comes to you in church as you kneel waiting for that sacred gift." Thomas thought in that case he would likely almost be unable to contain his excitement at the appropriate time.

Matua asked where his clothes were.

"Oh, the Māori boys don't go to chapel with the other children," Matron explained with unexpected softness.

"You have your own church service later today, in your own language."

That all sounded reasonable, except that when Thomas came downstairs there was Alf, standing by the doorway to chapel. He carried a swagger stick, just like Mr James'.

The younger children cringed as they passed.

Inside, the chapel was bare. No statues of saints. Thomas understood this, that was the Protestant way. But no altar table either. "Into your seat. Hurry up." Matron slapped him on the side of his head, so that it ached. Why do people keep doing that when they know it hurts, he thought?

"Please?" he asked, slipping into his bench as he was told but tugging at her skirt.

"What?"

"Where do we kneel to receive the Blessed Sacrament?"

Her eyes bulged. "What did you just say?"

"The Blessed Sacrament, miss. Holy Communion. Father Murphy said it was all right to receive it in a Protestant church if we couldn't get to one of our own."

Her bosom trembled as if she had just heard him utter a profanity. "And who, pray,

boy, is Father Murphy?"

"He's our priest."

She leant forward. He could smell her breath. It was not a good smell. It reminded him of rotting eggs. Now she spoke very gently, stressing the sibilants. "Isss he, and are you, by any chancssse a member of the Church of Rome?"

Thomas thought about it. "That must be it, I think, miss. The Roman Catholic church. That's what it says on our chapel signboard."

A sly smile of triumph. As if she had a flyswat, and he was an annoying fly. Then he was being dragged outside the chapel, to where Alf was picking his nails and affably watching a tearful little boy beg to be pardoned for having a tear in his breeches.

"Alf, I want you to use that strong arm of yours to teach

this boy so he can't sit down for a week. I want him brought into a better understanding of the evil of the church within which he is raised, and the proper and necessary spiritual work of the Christian Mission in refusing to use such blasphemous and dangerous tricks as the so-called Holy Sacraments again. Unless he wants to spend time in the cellar explaining his profane theology to the rats."

"Right you are, Matron. But he'll have to stand in line until I have finished with little Jimmy here. Second time in a week Jimmy's come to church parade improperly dressed."

Jimmy gave a wail. "It's not my fault – it's the other boys – they're bullying me – they tear my clothes-"

Alf sniggered. "All the better to thrash you through. You see, Matron. I got my work cut out for me here this morning."

Matron shrugged. "Take your time. It will do the little Papist good to wait."

At that moment, Thomas saw Matua being dragged by two armed constables down the stairs.

A powerful rage overtook him. "What's happening?" He started to move forward.

Alf and Matron moved, pincer-like, to hold him against the wall. He struggled.

"You lied to me – you said he was coming to chapel later –"

"He's a traitor, Thomas," said Alf smoothly. "Confessed it to me. Tried to get me on his side. Made a big mistake he did, thought I was a rebel Māori Kingite instead of a loyal Queenie....."

Thomas gave an impassioned roar. "Stop it! Don't listen to them! It's not true! He's not an enemy agent! He's my friend!"

One of the constables gave him a quick, sympathetic glance. The iron gates clanged open. One constable led Matua out, another shut the gate behind him. There was a horrible pause.

"Oh, I'm afraid it is true." Matron tucked her bonnet ribbons back and dusted her hair. "Your little friend and his tribe have been planning an armed assault on Auckland for months. He confided it all to good loyal Alf, here – the plan to sail up the Manukau harbour, and set alight to the city from within." She gave a theatrical shudder. "Why, I imagine if we had not discovered the plot we would shortly all have been murdered in our beds."

Alf whistled, and stuck his cap back on his head. "Reckon Governor Grey won't have any choice but to go to war now, don't you think? What a pity, when he was so keen on keeping peace. Them Kingites will be getting a bloody nose before too long." They both laughed.

"Well," Matron smiled at them both, "I had better go and superintend the pupils in chapel."

Thomas took a deep breath. Now was his chance.

Watching, he had noticed that the constabulary had exited the iron gates and shut it behind them. The porter outside was chatting to a passerby. The gate was shut, but not yet locked.

He let out a loud, theatrical sob.

Alf snorted. As Thomas had hoped, he bent down close. "If you think that kind of snivelling will get you out of a sound hiding – "

Desperate measures, but there was a time and place. He kicked Alf in the groin, as hard as he could. He saw the boy flinch and crumple, then collapse on the ground.

He gave Alf another kick in the stomach to make sure he could not get up for a few more seconds, and began to sprint towards the street.

Jimmy gave a wail. "Wait! Let me go too!"

He couldn't take him. But he had to. He had no choice.

Jimmy's voice, calling out like his little brother, on the ship, crying out for better food. No one had listened from the upper classes on the ship. He'd begged and begged but no one would stop and help. Now there was a little grave in Onehunga. This boy's cheeks were sunken in the same ominous way. There might be enough food to go around, but it wasn't being shared fairly. Probably the reason those older pupils looked so healthy was that they were in charge of distribution. It was a simple Darwinian question of survival of the fittest. They needed to survive, so they would be eating it all. The younger children were being left to starve. Jimmy would die too, if he stayed here.

Cursing, Thomas picked him up roughly and ran for the gate. Heavy as a parcel of bricks, and just as useless to me, he thought bitterly. I'm a sentimental fool and when I don't get away it'll be because I tried to save this little urchin too.

He never knew how he managed it, perhaps it was all the hurling games he had played as a boy at home. Perhaps no one ever tried to escape, so they were not used to it. Whatever the reason, he managed to dodge the senior students who poured out of the chapel after him, and the elderly porter who staggered out from the other side of the gate. Someone shouted "Stop thief!" but it was Sunday morning and the streets were empty. Before Alf could recover enough to chase him, Jimmy and he were outside, panting, a hundred yards out of sight down the road.

2019

Hamilton

Another nightmare.

Ben opened his eyes, and stared depressedly at the random patterns of light on the tiled ceiling. The curtains were poorly designed, and did not quite cover the whole window. That wouldn't have been so bad, the windows only led to a corridor, lit day and night with artificial fluorescent strips. Any nurse or orderly or relative who passed could stop and gape.

Goldfish bowl, that's what it was. No privacy, any more than a good night's sleep.

You might as well stick him in a cell and be done with it.

He tried to turn over and rest. But his heart was still racing from the nightmare.

Calm down, first. Then sleep. But how?

The proper way, he knew, was prayer. *Though I walk through the valley of the shadow of death.* But did he fear evil, really? The visions he was having were glorious and intangible. But they were also – obviously – rubbish, the result of a disordered mind. Is that what all the Old Testament prophets had been doing, having seizures and telling people about them? He'd been allowing himself to think these things more clearly in hospital. Rosemary's incessant warbling in tongues had sounded more and more like nonsense and less like divinely inspired sacred speech. At night it was less comfortable. The gaping hole of blackness that was the universe. Monkeys clinging to a rock, that's all they were. Death was itself, not a doorway to a better place. If a virus came and wiped humanity out, that would just be the pattern of existence, and not a judgement of the Lord that could be prayed away. All very intellectually coherent – and in the daytime, it felt as if a straightjacket had been lifted off his brain - but not as placidly comforting as psalms. Especially when you were trying to get back to sleep.

A wank would help, but Ben was acutely conscious of the busy corridor and the gaps in the curtains. Perhaps a glass of water. The orderly had poured one before leaving him for the night.

"Finest waters of the Waikato, all piped and treated ready for your honour," he had told him with a grin. He was a good guy, he didn't just do the basics for your body but also chatted to you like a real person. It made you feel better just talking to him.

He tested to see if his hands were working. Sometimes they didn't, during or just after a seizure. Yes, all seemed fine. He sat up, and reached for the glass of water. Then a sudden spasm took him, and his right hand knocked over the glass. Water splashed everywhere, over the portable table and his bed,

Fuck, fuck, fuck. He tasted the words on his tongue, trying to get used to the flavour. There was a frisson, a sort of power to them. Swearwords were like strong alcohol, his father had confided in him once, when his mother was out of the room: you might end up tasting them occasionally but best not to get into the habit. Fuck it felt good, though. Fuck, shit, damn and blast. Bollocks to you all. The words poured out of him. Shit goddam fuck you all to hell. A river of profanity, water on the face of the deep. He felt better, like he'd been constipated for ages and finally emptied his bowels. But the sheets were still wet. Grimacing, he reached for the buzzer.

It took them a while to get to him. He wasn't an

emergency case, he knew, and sometimes there were dozens of patients who all needed the toilet at once. He tried to bear with this placidly, knowing his young bladder was stronger than many of the old gents on the ward, but it could get uncomfortable sometimes, and today when he was cold and shivering it was awful.

They came, eventually. When the first nurse saw what had happened he called two caregivers to help him. They weren't angry at all that he'd made a mess, for which he was grateful. He was trying not to be a bother, but shit it was difficult when you couldn't move or walk. A chrysalis life, that was what he had now. Sludgy and sweating, trapped in a hospital bed. Swearing was the only superpower he had left, now he'd accepted finally and for all that prayer would never work.

The sheets were changed whilst he shivered on the commode. He jerked and rolled a bit but one nurse held him so he didn't fall. Then it was on with the new pyjamas, and back into bed. The nurse and one caregiver left, and he was left with the kind one who had joked with him about the water earlier.

"Right, anything else you need?"

Ben grimaced. "Just need to wipe up that table. It's my homework."

"Some of these papers got a bit wet. Not badly, but let's spread them out to dry.

What are they?" The caregiver looked at them in puzzlement.

"Oh, it's family history stuff. We're doing a project." Ben would like to have said more, but he was aware other patients were probably waiting for the toilet. Part of him wanted to try out being selfish, now that he wasn't interested in pleasing the Almighty any more, but he also wanted to prove his parents wrong that no one who didn't fear the judgement of hell could possibly be unselfish and good.

"Nice. Good to work hard in school. Otherwise you'll

end up in slave labour like me."

The caregiver spread them out on the newly dried table with the same brisk, careful approach he took to all his duties. He gave Ben a final wink - "no wild parties now" - and left the room.

"Yeah. When I can't even walk."

"You will. Just wait until they get you on those meds. You'll be fine."

The reminder that all this suffering was probably unnecessary made Ben want to howl. He breathed deeply, allowing himself the new luxury of allowing himself to feel fury at God for giving him such stupid anti-medical parents. Which meant, shit, perhaps he wasn't totally atheist yet. Perhaps part of him needed to believe in a God, even an evil one. He was so conditioned into faith that he had to believe in a universal mastermind.

It would take a while to train himself out of the mental habits of belief.

"I hate you," he said to God, experimentally. The world did not end.

Ben looked around the new idea of a world that had not been created. Everything seemed sharper, somehow, sort of fresh and new. It was hot, though, and the papers on the table were already half-dried.

Something caught his eye. That was odd.

The photograph hadn't been much damaged by the water, just a small splash in the top corner, a drop that now hung like a random cloud in the sky. But as if that splash had somehow altered the very substance and being of the scene, the picture itself had changed. The schoolhouse, pupils and river backdrop were unchanged, but the pupils sat without a tutor. The man who had somehow come forward in time to kidnap Adele - and who, Ben was starting to suspect, was also connected to the Mr James who wrote those crafty spying letters - had, when splashed by the Waikato waters, completely disappeared. And the letter which could not possibly have been written by Sheila was now a blank page.

South Auckland, 2019

A full belly was good, but it wasn't enough. Adele walked along the edge of the Takanini motorway, wondering where to spend the night.

There. On a black guardrail. Railings, like she'd seen in the old London films (before they were all melted down for aircraft in the wad). A small, unobtrusive sign. "Salvation Army. Emergency and transitional housing. Please ring doorbell for help."

She knew a bit about the Salvation Army. Every now and again, Cynthia would take her there. Not often, because the food parcels were unappetising, but when life home educating without any child maintenance or income other than the Domestic Purposes Benefit got too financially tough. Generally it was because the car had broken down again, and WINZ were refusing any emergency assistance because they'd had their loan and food grant allocation for the year already. Adele was never allowed inside the room where Cynthia would go and, as she put it,

"Humbly apologise and be told off for being poor. I don't need you to see me doing this," she said quite sharply when Adele once asked why she could not come inside, "I am obliged to do it because we need this food today and there is no other way I can get it. I would prostitute myself literally if it meant you could eat so I think I can bear a degrading conversation with the Salvation Army. But there's no reason why I have to let them humiliate me in front of you."

Cynthia was rarely sharp, so Adele was surprised. But, she reasoned now, Cynthia was also quite picky.

Why, she had had a row with the Woman's Refuge when they were there because

the toys were broken and unsafe, the clothes they gave them ragged and there were cockroaches in the kitchen. Cynthia felt that all these things were inappropriate for a publicly funded organisation. Adele personally felt that her father was horrible enough that a few cockroaches and broken toys were a small price to pay for the opportunity to get rid of him.

So she felt the Salvation Army were probably worth a try, particularly as whatever Cynthia said they were like in the private meetings they were always kind and cheerful to her whilst she waited in the front room, and at the fundraising Christmas Carols outside Kmart the old man carrying the bucket was nothing short of delightful.

"Can we give him money, please?" Adele would nag her mother.

"No. They're a cult. Worse than the Catholics. And that's saying something."

Adele rolled her eyes. Her mother was ridiculous sometimes.

"Mum. It's money for the poor."

"We are the poor. And they bully us."

"How do I know that when you won't let me in the room?"

" Stop it. I won't have this argument again."

But they did, every year.

Adele straightened her shoulders, reminded herself that her mother would also have been suspicious of the perfectly kind and unthreatening Sikhs, and rang the bell.

A sharp-eyed social worker answered. Or at least, social worker was what her name tag said. ("Did it say registered social worker?" asked her mother, later, when she heard the story. "Thought not.") She unlocked the gate with a button, and held it half open, as if afraid Adele might try to break inside.

Adele explained awkwardly that she had nowhere to sleep tonight. The social worker hesitated.

"How old are you?"

Adele crossed her fingers.

"Sixteen."

The social worker looked at her disbelievingly. "Really?"

"Yes."

"Do you have a faith?"

Adele was fairly sure from what her mother had said that the Salvation Army were not supposed to ask this as a precondition to offering help, but what was she supposed to do? I can't say I am Christian, she thought, because they might ask me about Jesus. And I don't know anything, because religion is the one subject we never did at home. She plumped for a plausible alternative. "Jewish." The social worker looked mildly interested.

"Messianic? I mean, do you believe in Our Lord?"

"Jesus? No." She knew that Mark and Sheila did not. "I mean, we believe that he existed as a human being. But not.." She wavered, trying not to betray her ignorance... "anything else."

The social worker sighed disapprovingly, and held the gate a little more tightly shut.

"What's your name?"

"Christina Rosetti." It was the first name that she could think of. Help, I've just given the name of a famous poet, she thought. She tried again. "Rosetta, I mean. Christina Rosetta."

"And do you have some form of identification? A doctor's letter, addressed to you, for example? Or a driver's licence?"

Adele shook her head.

"No. I couldn't take anything when I ran away. I didn't have time. My dad, he threatened to kill me." That, at least, was true.

The social worker sighed, and looked very tired. "You have to go through WINZ. We don't take anyone unless they can pay rent, and rent has to be sorted through WINZ if you're under eighteen. You're a minor. Anyway, I'm sorry, we're full."

Adele started to wonder what the charitable aspect was of an organisation that demanded rent to give shelter to the homeless, until she remembered Cynthia grumbling that the Women's Refuge did the same. "You would think they would understand that when you have left everything you own and are in traumatic shock it might be helpful to have two or three nights, at least, of genuine hospitality. Without having to beg and plead for so much as a free toothbrush."

"If I go to WINZ they'll just send me back home."

"Not if you're really sixteen."

Adele took a deep breath, and remembered her mother's comments about prostitution. "All right, fair enough. But if you don't let me in, at least for tonight, I'm going to go back down that road there and get in the car with the first man who offers me a bed. Is that what you want?"

"Fair doos, kid. You'd better come in."

2019

Hamilton

Moses was the hospital chaplain. He wasn't anything to do with Oranga Tamariki, he promised. Moses by name and Moses by nature, the consultant said proudly, "he's a friend to us all. Great man. If I had a problem, I'd want to talk to Moses."

Moses came from a small island off the coast of Fiji. Epilepsy happens there, he said, but most of the time we don't have medicine for it. So boys like you just have to suffer. Ben shuddered at the thought of spending the rest of his life needing help to pee.

Moses was quite happy to sit and talk to Ben about whatever Ben wanted, which was definitely not epilepsy or religion or his parents. Rosemary was still in Auckland. The church was funding a lawyer for them to fight their case, not that there was a case yet, but it was obvious that if they didn't give way soon Oranga Tamariki and the hospital were going to end up applying to court to order Ben to be treated.

Moses wondered how Ben felt about life in general, and whether there were any other issues bothering him, or if he would rather they just caught up once a day and had a general chat and maybe a game of cards. Ben thought the game of cards was a splendid idea. So Moses brought a pack of cards and taught Ben how to play rummy. The Oranga Tamariki woman turned up once or twice with her spiky hair and tried to join in, but Moses suggested that she come back another time.

After about four days of rummy, Ben asked Moses why he was a Christian. Moses said he was. "I'm not sure I ever decided one way or another. It's just, at home church is everywhere. It's a part of everyday life." Ben asked if he believed in creation or evolution. Moses said he thought he rather believed in both. "Different eras have different stories for how their world came to be," he mused. "Which make sense for the world they live in, and the people they need to be. And sometimes different people, even in the same families, can live in different worlds."

Ben hesitated. "What about gay people?" Moses laughed. "Before the Bible came to Fiji, gay love was not a problem. I am not going to condemn my ancestors for doing what came naturally at the time. They didn't have the Bible then, so what were they to do?" Ben liked the way Moses could hold together so many different ways of seeing the world at once. But he also found it irritating. If the Bible didn't have all the answers, what was the point of using it to mess up people's lives by laying down random rules?

"I think I'm gay," he said aloud. Moses shrugged. "Then that's who you are. You'd better find a way of being you."

The vanished photograph lay on the table. It had gradually leached away its colour, so that there was nothing left. Tentatively, Ben raised the subject of demons. "Do people in Fiji believe in that? Do you?"

"Who knows," Moses said after a pause. "Some do, in my village. Some don't. Sometimes I think evil is supernatural, and sometimes it is in the DNA, or medical. A disordered brain. Then sometimes it is the person choosing to be evil all on their own. But most of the time it is a mixture of all." He laughed. "You ask interesting questions,

Ben. You have a good mind. I will miss you, when they let you out."

"Let me out? I'm in a fucking prison, aren't I?"

He hadn't tried swearing in a normal conversation yet.

It felt good.

Moses laughed, ruefully. "You're here to be healed. Isn't that what prison is? Or at least, what it's meant to be?"

I bet it's not, though, thought Ben. I bet it's just a pious sham like everything else.

He didn't say that aloud. It wasn't Moses' fault that he was still naïve enough to believe in God.

1862

The Parliament Buildings
Auckland

"But I don't understand why you say there is nothing you can do. You are a respected senior politician. An expert in Native Affairs."

"It's no use, Vogel. Grey and Cameron are absolutely bent on war with the Māori at all costs. Parliament can do nothing against them. Believe me, we have tried."

Frederick Weld, Member for the Cheviot district, warmed his legs against the hotel fire. He looked fondly at his old friend.

"I'm so glad you remembered me. It is good to catch up. Such a long time since we saw each other in London."

Vogel nodded. "Good men of good intent must stick together in times like these. I should tell you, I was in the gallery watching when you put forward that very brave amendment – that attempt to prevent the new Parliament opening in an Anglican prayer –"

Weld sighed. "Doomed, of course. But as a Catholic I had to try. For ourselves, and all the other denominations. And you and your fellow Jews too of course."

"Yes. Who knows, if the Empire continues to blow fast ships along the trade winds, one day maybe even Hindus, Muslims and Sikhs will come to Auckland to live. They will need fair representation in Parliament too. We cannot allow one church to dominate. Parliament must be for all the religions, and even those of no religion at all."

Vogel turned over the papers in front of him. Tiredness seeped through him with the Auckland winter damp. The ship bringing him up from Otago to Auckland had only docked two hours ago. But there was no time to waste.

"Here, Frederick. May I use your first name? I want you to see the article I pub-

lished in the Otago Daily Times. About the situation here."

Weld put on his glasses, and read with care. "This is by you? It's untitled."

"Yes. I can't be too overly partisan as the editor."

"Naturally."

Weld nodded approval. "It's good. Fiery, but good. You should consider a career in politics."

"I – a practising Jew – impossible."

"You never know."

"I mean they say Disraeli may soon be Prime Minister in Britain. But he for the sake of political advancement has abandoned his principles and embraced the Christian Faith."

"Auckland is not London. The people dislike too much discrimination amongst their fellow Anglo Saxons. As long as you are not Māori , you have a fair crack of the whip."

"Well, and about the Māori question, this is really why I am here. I did not sail for two months from Otago to discuss my own political aspirations." Vogel smiled wearily. "I suffer seasickness far too readily for that."

Weld sat down heavily in his plush chair. Too plush for today, he thought, we should be kneeling in desperate beseeching to the Almighty on a hard stone floor. "Well, I have bad news for you I am afraid. I am of the opinion that you have arrived about a day too late. It was entirely possible in principle that the toothless, powerless, unrepresented New Zealand Parliament might be at the very least able to delay the inevitable decision to go to war until we had, at the very least, appealed for a steadier pair of hands from the British Colonial Office. But not as of now."

He poured a glass of wine.

"Drink this. You'll need it."

Vogel groaned.

"Then tell me the worst and let me bear it like a man. Don't leave me in the agony of suspense."

Weld began to explain how a plot had just been uncovered. A native princeling had been brought to the city for the sake of education, and had confided to a subject of the Queen how the southern tribes had come to see the building of the road as itself an unbearable provocation. They had determined to attack first, and he was to take his opportunity and set fire to the city from within.

Vogel went white. "The worst of all possible worlds. How could the Māori leadership have been so foolish as to countenance this?"

"No idea. I have sent word to our man the Quartermaster at Pokeno. He is of our league, and carries regular messages to the King and his warriors. He swears he has heard nothing of it until now. He does not believe it is true. He met the boy himself, and says he heard nothing amiss. He is of the strong view that it is all a putup job."

"I see. And what do you feel?"

Weld slammed his hand on the table in frustration. "I agree with him. But they will torture the boy, if they have not done so already. He is only a lad. There will be a show trial, and a slow hanging of course. Everything that can possibly be done to inflame the Māori into war. Possibly by the New Year." He fought for words. "Forgive me my Catholic love of symbol. I feel as if New Zealand today is like the pohutakawa tree. So grey and green and peaceful, but about to burst into Christmas flames."

Vogel shoved the paperwork aside impatiently. "Or like the pohutakawa bark. You strip it what looks a natural everyday colour, to find crimson bloodsap flowing underneath. This is bad news. Worse than I feared. I thought we had a year. Give me wine."

He drank.

"Is there anything that can be done?"

"Only if we can find his companion. A young Irish lad. Blunt thinks he may be able to give vital evidence. But of course, nothing is ever so simple."

"Don't tell me. He's dead."

"Not yet. He's disappeared. Wise lad. He ran away. But they've put out a Wanted call for him as an accomplice. Of course, he won't be found. Not officially, at least. I have little doubt that they will murder him as soon as they get hold of him, unless by the grace of the One to whom we don't wish to pray in Parliament we manage to find him first."

2019

Mangere Village

I'd almost talked myself into thinking Thin-Lips wouldn't cause any harm. Too many people around, and all of us looking out for the kids. But the next morning, there he was. Some poor little guy splashing in puddles, off on his own and Thin-Lips coming up to him and telling him he was a good boy. Saying he knew some better puddles round the corner. That gentle voice, the way he'd started with me.

I ran up and grabbed his arm.

"I know what you're up to. Leave him alone."

He swings away from the kid. Looks at me with those cold pebbly eyes. A moment of confusion, then he places me. A grim smile plays along the edges of his thin lips.

"Oh look, well, isn't it Hape."

"You get out of here. Stop messing around."

He laughed. "I'm here to survey the site. Police orders. What are you going to do? Hape by name, Hape by nature, aren't you. Always the sulker, always left out, always on your own. You loved it when I locked you in that cupboard, do you remember? All in the dark by yourself, just like Hape when he got abandoned in Hawaiiki. No family, no friends. No one to stick up for you."

I was too angry to speak. He took it for weakness, rattled on.

"That's why you showed up here, isn't it? Out of work, nothing to do, no friends. Don't give me that you care about the whenua line. You're here because you're lonely and bored. Lads like you, they just roam the world forever, looking for somewhere to belong."

He always talked. I remember that. More words than anyone would think possible come out of that tightlipped thin mouth. Verbal diarrhoea, just like when he locked me in the cupboard and I crapped myself with fear.

"Haven't you grown? You look so tough. Bet you've talked yourself into a right

state, haven't you? Psyched yourself up, if you ever saw me again you'd beat my brains out. But you know what, you're not going to do anything. Because you know what I did to you, we both know it can't be undone. And killing me won't fix that. Will it? It'll just create more of a bloody mess."

Somehow he'd walked me to the edge of the field. Away from the other protesters.

"Go on. Show me you're a man, Hape. Hit me. Hit me, hard as you want, and then I'll call the police. Make a big deal out of it. Go on. Hit me and we'll have our violent protestor story. It's what the council want. It's what the building company want. And it's what I want too. So go on, be a man and take a swing. Trust me, it'll make my day."

I looked at the ground.

"Yeah, you're all the same. What, you reckon you're a big boy now? You think you're brave, because you survived me. But I know the truth. Only the cowardly kids ever let me away with it. You never fought back, did you? Not once. Candy-ass. Big girl's blouse. Look at you, making out so macho. But underneath you're just a pussy girl."

His words kicked me in the gut. For a moment I couldn't see, just the way when you've been hit on the head. Of course, he was right. I was a girl. Just not in the way he meant. But that didn't mean I couldn't hit him.

I looked up. No sound of footsteps. But he was gone.

I reported him to the Wardens, of course. That was all I could do. I dunno why I didn't think of it sooner. But it was too late now, he'd left the site. Probably come back tomorrow and try it on with some other poor kid.

All I could do, was go down to the entrance and be on guard duty. Borrowed one of the army blankets they had in the storepile. Wrapped it around myself. Not as good as a jacket in the rain, but it'd have to do.

I'd stand there until the protest ended, if it stopped him getting near another kid again.

2019

South Auckland

Adele looked around the bedroom. It looked pleasant, if bare. Not full, then, she thought.

This would be all right for a couple of days. It was Friday now, and they had said she could stay until Monday morning. Then they would take her down to WINZ offices to confirm her identity. That would obviously be disastrous, so she would have to leave before then. Perhaps she could go north, hitchhike to Kaitia where Granma lived.

The thought of seeing Granma was so precious that it made a sob judder in her stomach. Granma, with her white tablecloths and two candles on a Friday evening. ("I don't know why we do it," she'd said, "But my grandmother was married to one of those Port Jews and he liked it, that was all"). Granma, with her toothless smile and the horses she still kept on her field even though she was too old to ride them. Perhaps, she thought, perhaps if I do get up to her and explain what has happened, we can go and see the police together. Perhaps they will let me stay living with her.

But for now she needed to sleep and wash. And if possible find a way to get some money.

There was a timid knock on the door. This was a surprise because the social worker had explained that if she was to stay there she would have to understand that she was On A Programme and There Were Rules. One of those rules was silence at night, and another one of those rules was curfew.

This seemed to break both of those at once. Adele opened it, gingerly.

"I'm sorry to bother you." The woman – a couple of years older – smiled apologetically. "I'm Judy. I need some help changing my bedsheets. We have to do it once a week."

Adele saw she had a withered arm and leg. "Sure," she said, automatically. "No problem." They walked along the corridor. Or at least, Adele walked. Judy dragged herself painfully.

The bedsheets were waiting to be changed in a clean pile. The room was almost eerily clean. A few bags of what looked like clothes were piled against the walls, as if the occupant was frightened to take them out. Adele changed the bedsheets. It was a simple job.

"Thank you so much. I was worried I would get into trouble." Judy was almost in tears. Adele was about to tell her not to be so silly, but then she thought of some of the other odd things she had noticed that afternoon, whilst she had been sitting in the front office.

There had been the old man who had come in for his weekly meeting. Apparently you had to have one of those, if you lived here, so that you could prove you were looking for work and also looking for somewhere to live. He was, the Salvation Army accepted, too old for work, but there was no reason why he could not volunteer in their stores. He agreed to that. It didn't sound much like he was being given much choice. Not volunteering at all, then.

"What if I'm just too tired to manage it? I mean my health is not so good."

"You absolutely don't have to," his young social worker reassured him. "It's just that if you don't meet our requirements of a weekly life skills session and volunteer work you won't get the food parcel."

The old man sagged, and promised he would do his best to turn up.

Halfway through the meeting he'd apologetically asked

if he could use the toilet. The social worker had explained that was out of the question, this was a staff toilet and residents must go back to their own block. The old man shuffled painfully out. Adele was about to ask what the hell would happen to their precious staff toilet if he was allowed to use it, but then she remembered she was in urgent need of a bed.

Then there had been the young woman who had been thrown out. She'd sworn quite a lot, especially as she had nowhere to go and had only missed one weekly meeting. But she didn't have a good excuse, and had no evidence that she was looking for alternative accommodation or work. That was it. Out. No appeal.

There'd been another girl who'd been given a final warning. She'd disobeyed a rule too, but this was the one about not bringing in visitors. There must be no outsiders on the property at any time. It was her birthday, and her mother wanted to visit. She'd come in by car and for whatever reason the security guard on the gate hadn't noticed that she wasn't a resident. That was not anyone's fault, but the problem was that the daughter had not immediately escorted her off the premises. She had let her own mother sit in the bedroom with her and had even made a cup of tea. The security cameras had picked it up, of course. She had been hauled in and asked how she felt about putting other residents' safety at risk. This must not happen again.

The social workers also seemed obsessed with controlling the carpark. This was easy, because there were security cameras there as well. In fact, there were so many screens and cameras watching the residents at all times that Adele began to feel she was in an Orwellian movie.

One resident was called into the office and told to repark her car so that it faced the same way as the other resident cars. She asked what difference it made, and pointed out that some of the staff were parking their cars the wrong way around. That was apparently none of her business and she should watch her attitude.

Next the office staff discussed at length the problem of a car that had not been moved for a week. They were not a storage facility, they pointed out. Residents should not be encouraged to have property they did not need. Perhaps they would be benevolent for now, and give the resident another twenty four hours before calling the towing company. But this situation must not be allowed to continue. A car could not simply sit there, not doing anything to earn its keep.

They were interrupted by the middle-aged resident who came politely to the door and stood on the step to ask for more cleaning rags. There was only one in her unit, and she didn't want to cross-contaminate by using the same for kitchen and bathroom. The housekeeper told her sharply not to be silly, there were plenty in her unit. She protested that there was not, and the housekeeper quickly shut the door. Perhaps that, Adele thought, was why the residents were forced to stand outside on the path and talk to staff in public about their problems, if they needed help. It was humiliating and embarrassing so that that no one approached the staff unless they really needed to. It also meant that a difficult conversation could be ended with a quick slam of the door.

Adele was by this time thoroughly terrified, but she knew she needed a place to sleep. Just for a couple of days, she whispered to herself, sitting on the office chair. Just a couple of days.

But the most alarming conversation she had overheard in the office was an urgent staff meeting held about a resident who needed carers. Perhaps this was Judy. She hoped not. Because the social workers were adamant that they were not going to let her have people to support her come into the premises. It was An Exception and it would Set A Bad Example. Other residents might want visitors, if

Judy was allowed people inside to help her wash and dress.

"What if she asks about disability and human rights?" One social worker asked.

The door to their office was ajar. Adele listened attentively.

"She won't. She's got nowhere else to go."

"You never know. She might kick up trouble –"

"We just show them our lovely disabled facilities. Those big bathrooms. That should demonstrate how much we care."

There was a rumbled laugh.

"Yes, the ones that unfortunately have been built in buildings that have doors too small to access a wheelchair..."

Now she remembered it. The cnverastions that made no sense, unless they were deliberately trying not to help. Unless they were trying to drive Judy out.

"I'm not sure why you think you might get into trouble.." she asked hesitantly. Judy laughed bitterly. "Sit down. Let me tell you how this place works."

Adele sat.

"The Salvation Army have operated for over a hundred years on the principle that if you are poor and homeless it is your fault. Now there's a homelessness crisis in Auckland, plenty of people without a house through no fault of their own, but they're still behaving as if all you need to get a roof over your head is a short sharp shock."

Adele nodded, guardedly. This sounded like Cynthia. She didn't disbelieve it, necessarily, but she wasn't going to swallow it at face value either.

"Look at what you're sitting on. Comfortable, is it?"

Adele saw the point. There was no soft furniture in the room. Now she thought about it, there was no soft furniture anywhere in the complex, except for the room where the social workers had their meetings with residents. Their bottoms were obviously precious enough to need cushions, but not the, the, no. Not the inmates. She wasn't in prison.

Although it was true, they were locked inside at night. Perhaps more of an open prison, where you were allowed outside to work.

"Check in the morning. Outside. See if there is anywhere you can relax here, with other residents. There's nothing. Just washing lines. Industry, hard work, that's what they want here. No communal space except the kitchen. No lounge. It's all new, purpose built. Its prison style. Done on purpose. They don't want us socialising or making friends. We're supposed to sit in our rooms by ourselves. Easier to control. And have you noticed there's no wifi? That's to make it harder to look for work or accommodation here. So you have to go out every day, to the library or the benefit office, as if you're going to work."

Adele hoped she was hearing paranoia, but it sounded awfully like the organisation Cynthia had described.

"Which is fine, if you are healthy enough. But some of us aren't. And they throw you out if you're not fit. I'm not allowed carers to come in, and they fined me eighty dollars last week because I didn't change the bedsheets." Adele gulped. Eighty dollars. That was what Cynthia and she spent on food for a week.

She went back to her room. The door to the bathroom was unexpectedly locked. Shrugging, she went to the kitchen, found a saucepan and peed in it. Then she threw it out of the window. Take that, Salvation Army, she thought. I'd rather be on the streets.

She'd leave first thing in the morning.

A knock on the door.

"Who is it?" she asked guardedly.

An awkward cough. "Police."

1862

Auckland Central

My waters contain so many corpses. I am the bringer of life, and yet you constantly feed me death. The warriors at Rangitiri and Meremere that bled into the ground. The little boys and girls who play too frivolously in the current, so that they are pulled away by a strong West Coast wave. The surfers who do the same, and never make it back to shore.

Not everything ends badly in this story, though, and the reason is partly Jimmy. Little Jimmy, who did not know anything much except how to beg, and had a finely honed sense for who might be worth begging from.

Like any successful child beggar, he was sweet and persistent. He was also truly grateful to Thomas, and happy to do his best to provide for them both. That was how it came to be little Jimmy who ran up to Weld and Vogel as they left the hotel from their depressing consultation, begging for a bite to eat.

Vogel looked at him with dislike.

"Is this a new Auckland problem, Frederick? I don't remember seeing child beggars last time I was here."

"New enough," Weld jingled the money in his pocket. "Boy, who do you beg for? I don't like giving to children who pretend they are on their own. There is always an older man or woman behind them. A Fagin, if you will excuse the expression, Julius."

Jimmy pointed to where Thomas stood, a few feet away.

Weld started. "Good Lord. Julius."

"What?"

"Boy, what is your name? Answer me honestly, and don't try to run away."

"Thomas, sir. Thomas Fenton. Of Port Waikato, sir."

Weld gave a sigh of relief. "Dear heavens. I thought so. You resembled the boy in the description Blunt gave us. But I was uncertain, until you spoke, and I heard the brogue. Come."

Thomas hesitated. This felt like a trap. A small crowd had gathered. He could probably get away, if he tried.

"Please." Vogel put his face close to Thomas' and whispered. "We need to act fast. Before they kill your friend."

2019

Auckland

The woman police officer listened attentively. Adele thought she probably believed her. There were the bruises, which helped, and the fact she had actually run away. But also, this woman just looked like she cared. She was blonde and young, with an impish smile. "I'll be honest with you," she confided after a few minutes, "I hate these Family Court cases and so do most of my colleagues. Ripping kids away from parents is not why we came into the police force."

"I do have to take you into custody," she went on, "but given what you have just disclosed about your father's behaviour tonight I don't have to return you to him. In fact I think I might lose my job if I did. Does that help?"

Adele nodded.

"What we'll do. We'll put you in the car and take you up to the station. You can make a formal statement about your father's assault and then he can be arrested and charged. Your mother has been deemed an unsuitable and unsafe carer – Yes, I know, but I'm not in charge of this lunatic system – so the chances are you will be put into social services custody for a few weeks, until the case goes before a judge. It's not perfect. But it's better than being on the streets."

Adele agreed with that. But there was one more question. "School?"

"Yes. I should think so." The police officer wrinkled her nose in distaste. "Couldn't stand it myself. Left as soon as I could. But we can't do anything about that for now."

Adele walked down the stairs. At least she was leaving the Salvation Army. From one prison to another. She couldn't tell if she was sorry or relieved.

At the sight of the police car, she flinched. Remembering Acne and Tall, she jerked back. The elderly police officer lunged and caught her, before she had even decided if she was running away or not.

"Look, you're a sensible lass. I don't think there's any need for handcuffs. Do you think you could manage not to run away if I I hold your hand," the police officer suggested kindly.

Adele nodded. She gave one hand to the woman officer, who held it gently, as one might to a small child . Now she felt helpless and pathetic. But she didn't pull away. The police officer was right, it was a lunatic situation. But she couldn't keep running away forever. She didn't, she realised, want to be difficult for now. As long as she wasn't returned to her father.

But that was impossible. No judge in the world would do that.

1862

Auckland

Matua lay in the darkness below the Governor's residence and groaned.

He was not in pain yet. Not physically, at any rate. Grey had met with him in person and explained that there was only one course of action open to him if he wished to avoid terrible agony and extended torture. This was to sign a confession of conspiracy to rebellion and trust to the mercy of the British government.

Matua had, of course, politely declined this course of action. There had been a brief but unpleasant interlude where the Governor had asked his personal guards to explore with Matua the likelihood of his keeping his arms and legs unbroken if he did not do as he was asked. Fortunately, the armed constables who had delivered him were still in the vicinity. They pointed out with some asperity that they were not answerable to the Governor but to the young New Zealand Parliament. Which might not have much power yet, but was still an institution of considerable idealism and weighty opinion. Moreover, it was founded on sound British principles of fair play and justice. They did not believe the constabulary had been founded in order to condone torture, even in the case of such an obviously guilty party as this young Prince.

Greeted with this vociferous opposition to foul play, Grey mildly agreed that the young man instead be conducted to a guest room to wash and rest, and perhaps consider his options at leisure. Matua had few illusions about the Governor's intentions and was not at all surprised when the cellars turned out to be his lodging. He was also not surprised to be left there, alone, for several days, with just enough food and water to keep him sane and coherent. This was logical, if the Governor wanted to intimidate him into submission without the awkward mess of actually having to torture him in front of potential witnesses.

He was surprised when the groans began from the next cellar. He had been pretty sure that he had been the only prisoner brought down here in the past week, and that the door to the neighbouring room had been open and empty when he passed. Yet now he could hear dozens of Māori voices. They came and went, too, so that sometimes it seemed that there were many of them, and sometimes just one or two. After a while he decided that possibly they were ghosts, and this did not frighten him so much as reassure him, because it suggested that war had not broken out yet, and that these were not military prisoners.

"Rangitiri, Rangitiri." They said this often, so that their voices reverberated through the walls. They said it in a tone of pride, but also lament. What had happened there? Matua tried to think of anything noteworthy from the histories he had heard on the marae. But there was nothing. It took a couple more days before he reasoned that if they were ghosts, there was no reason why they had to be coming from the past. The Europeans had invaded New Zealand and technical development had sped forward a thousand years in a couple of decades. What if that very speed of cultural and social transformation had done something to the framework of time, so that whatever he was hearing might come, like the European technology, from the future? Rangitiri might be a battle the Māori were going to lose, rather than one they had already lost. These could be the ghosts of prisoners that had not yet been taken. Which was depressing, but ki te kahore he whakakitenga ka ngaro te iwi. Without foresight or vision the people will be lost. In European terms, forewarned is forearmed.

It was abundantly clear that the Waikato would shortly be at war. But least if he escaped he could prevent his father fighting at Rangitiri. And if not, and he was shortly put to death, then thinking about the changing direction of time that the Europeans had brought to his country was better than crying in the dark and pissing himself with fear.

Or thinking about what was to come. Matua knew perfectly well that he wasn't going to hold out for long. He'd always thought he was reasonably brave. Now, in the dark, he knew better. His eyes were wet and his bowels loose, just like the prisoners his grandfather had taken as slaves. Even the fiercest warriors would end up cowed after a few days.

He was no different. Probably the next time someone came into the cellar, he'd be begging them to let him out just long enough to betray his father and sign away his own life.

1864

Kawau

The water roared, and Sergeant Major Blunt came.

He rowed up the river to Kawau Island. When Vogel's *Otago Times* broke the scandal of what was happening on the ship, a transfer to the island was arranged. Kawau transfer gave them the new luxuries of light, fresh air and vegetables. There were even doctors to treat the sicknesses they had acquired on the ship. So it was with horror and disappointment that the *Weekly Auckland News* reported that a month or so later that the prisoners had refused to stay on the island and had shown typical "native character" in sneaking away to their families despite all the current luxuries of their confinement. The Colonial Administration loftily declared that they did not mind too much what happened to the escapees since they were costing a lot in sugar, flour, "and occasional sulphur." (Presumably for gunpowder to stop them escaping, or to shoot the odd miscreant).

This famous mass escape of 1864 is well recorded, unlike the minor matter of what the Auckland gossips in late 1862 termed the mysterious Māori prince and his Irish runaway servant. Governor Grey did indeed go to war, but he had to wait for another year. If there was a Māori plot to sack Auckland, it could never be proven. A taniwha can live by the river, a taniwha can be the river, a taniwha can live within the river. But a taniwha cannot betray the river, because that would be to betray its very soul. The hundred taniwhas of the Waikato and the hundred chiefs that knew Matua and his father closed ranks and refused to say a word as to how exactly Grey had been persuaded to let the young Māori hostage go.

Thomas did not say a word either, when he came back home to Port Waikato. There was a new teacher at the school, and a new vicar at the Anglican rectory. It was as though Mr James and Reverend Simpson had never been.

Jimmy came too. Thomas' family offered him a home. He stayed for a few weeks, and then left. He missed the city, he said apologetically. It was weird out here. Too quiet and green.

Matua and Thomas didn't like to talk much about what had happened when they were away. Thomas did say once to Father Murphy in Confession that he did not know if he had done wrong or not, but he had for the sake of a good friend tempted a great man of Auckland into nearly committing a terrible sin.

Father Murphy asked him if he could say a little more about it. Thomas described how Mr James had nearly treated him and Father Murphy got very angry and shouted that murder was too good for the likes of that one, and that there were some things he left to Our Lord to absolve, because he personally could not. Thomas got very worried then and tried to leave, but Father Murphy reassured him he was talking of the sins of adults, not of young boys.

So Thomas told the truth.

How that night they had all four of them, Vogel and Feld and Jimmy and he, waited outside Gray's residence until it was dark. Then Jimmy and he had gone and knocked on the door.

They had explained to the guards that they were bringing a personal package to the Governor and he would find the present they brought very enjoyable.

They were let in, and they waited a while. During that time they opened a window on the side of the house.

Quite soon, the Governor came to meet them. He was very friendly and kind. Jimmy and Thomas told him that they had been sent as a special present from his good friend Mr James, and Mr James had said to tell him that he hoped they would meet with his satisfaction. They asked which of them should get undressed first.

The armed constables who had arrested Matua and refused to let him be tortured had by then climbed through the windows and were waiting behind the elegantly ribboned curtains. When Governor Gray told Jimmy to take off his clothes, they leapt out and arrested him for indecency. He might not be subject to Parliament, they said, but even a Governor General must obey the law of the land.

Governor Gray blubbered a lot and spoke about scandal and how terrible this would be for his poor dear wife. The constables asked how Matua was doing and he was brought up hastily from the cellar. A deal was hastily cut, where the Governor agreed to let Matua go and take no more Waikato hostages. Moreover, the constables swore on their lives that he would be arrested and rot in jail if they ever heard of him fraternising with Mr James or spending time alone with young boys again.

"And that's how you persuaded him to let you go." Father Murphy breathed out sharply. "I had wondered. I knew James and Simpson were in the pocket of the Governor but I didn't realise that was what they were up to. Not with children."

"Yes. Did we do wrong?"

"Tempting him? Not at all. Needs must. You had to help your friend escape. Anyway, griends break the rules for each other. That's what friends do." Father Murphy's voice sounded choked. He took out a large handkerchief and blew his nose. "Sorry. Bit of a cold. Thank you for telling me this, Thomas. You can go now. No need to set any penances today."

Thomas uncurled his knees, and pushed open the

carved matau door. His thoughts clouded with a vague drift of anticlimax, he started to amble towards home. That was it, then. More farming. Maybe another year at school. He'd not get the chance to go travel again. Not that he wanted to, really.

Behind him, the gentle sound of the Waikato lapped reassuringly at the shore. As if nothing had happened worth the telling, and there was nothing new that could ever be said in the confessional at all. Life would go on, just as it had. You came back, and it was all as before. Even Jimmy had gone back to the life he knew.

Thomas pondered his future. He'd marry, soon enough, find a patch of scrub to clear. Maybe raise some sons, or daughters even. As long as he kept out of harm's way, and the war didn't come. The adventure was over. Nothing had changed. Except -

Turning on his heel, he swung back. Walking past the church, he set his eyes on the distant thatch of Matua's house. There was something he needed to do.

2019

Hamilton

To Ben's intense relief, the legal standoff did not get all the way to court. His parents had met with the expensive lawyer paid for by the church. He advised them not to hire him at all. Their chances of winning the case were miniscule, and if they persisted in refusing epilepsy treatment Ben would definitely be taken into care. The pastor advised them to stand firm in their faith and accept martyrdom of their son, just as the Father had done with his Son. Fortunately, that was the point where Rosemary realised there were limits to her holiness, and that perhaps allowing Ben to be treated was an allowable weakness of the maternal flesh that a loving Creator and Redeemer could forgive.

The medications worked. Ben was no longer having seizures. He'd also recovered from post-seizure psychosis. No more confused suicide attempts or unexpectedly slashed arms. At least, that was what the hospital diagnosed had been happening, based on the fact that Ben claimed not to have any recollection of previous events.

The cuts and bruises were pretty much healed. Ben thought it would probably be possible to stop himself doing it again once he was out. At least for a few days.

On his last morning in hospital, Moses stopped by to see him again.

"You're doing great, I'll miss our chats. Is there anything else you want to ask me?"

"Yes," Ben nodded. "There is. You know, my mother says

everything happens for a reason. And like so much else, I'm not sure what I believe any more."

Moses smiled. "Your epilepsy. It would be easier if it had happened for a reason. If it wasn't just random chance –"

Ben nodded again. It would. It was much easier to think of the universe as having purpose. Even if you weren't sure what or why that purpose was.

"If you were right, and your Mr James in that picture was a kind of demon," Moses articulated at length, "and if you were right, and he was a time traveller too. Then evil may travel through time, but so does love. Like the great craft, that travelled the Pacific, taking my people forwards and back."

The waka that brought Kupe. A powerful image. But Ben could not see quite what Moses meant, or why he thought it was important to say.

"Think of it like an arrow of light. Every time someone wills an action, good or bad, the universe is changed. So, whether you believe in a deity or not, if you are a good person, and you want to help people – then perhaps – just supposing, I mean like the epileptic youth on my island, or perhaps in the past, somewhere that medicine hadn't been invented yet. Perhaps someone had a terrible brain injury, or was even born with epilepsy, and their life would have been unbearable without the proper drugs." Moses sighed. "And yet they didn't develop epilepsy, and you did. For you, you see, it is the desert. And for them, the promised land."

"You mean like a gift? To suffer on behalf of someone else? Does that happen?"

Moses shrugged. "No one knows. I didn't say it happened. I said, or perhaps I didn't say but I think, that it may help you, just a little, now and then, to think of it in this way."

"You don't believe in God at all," burst out Ben. "You're just saying it's a nice idea." He slammed the bedrail in annoyance. "No wonder you don't care that I'm gay. You're an atheist, just like me."

Moses spread his hands out, appealingly. "And what if I am? Who wants to be a hairy ape, flying through space on a lonely rock? Isn't life easier when we think there's a point? So faith is a fiction, is taking comfort in fiction such a terrible thing? You can gain wisdom from a novel, even when you know the story isn't true."

"That's bullshit."

Moses regarded him sharply. "You know what's also bullshit? Knowing all the answers. Not asking for help. Leaving hospital, and starting to cut your arms again."

He folded his arms, and waited for a response.

Before Ben could recover himself and reply, Rosemary bustled in. "Good to see you're ready. Off we go. Dad's waiting in the car outside."

She'd brought clothes. Ben fumbled awkwardly into his outfit.. The scratchiness of Velcro and heavy polyester was almost uncomfortable against his skin. It was so long since he had worn anything since light hospital pyjamas.

"Bye." Moses spoke casually and ambled off up the corridor. All of a sudden he was blurry, through tears. The fluorescent lights flickered out. A sunlight shone on him, unexpectedly, so he seemed more water than man. A barrel of light seemed to pour itself out of nowhere, onto his fading head. Then he was gone. An empty corridor. But he hadn't reached the end.

Rosemary gave him a hug.

"Come on, funny fellow. Stop staring into space. It's not goodbye. It's hello." "I was saying goodbye to Moses."

"Who?

"The chaplain. You saw him. Just now."

Rosemary looked at him, puzzlement etched on her flabby face.

"What?"

"When you came in. We were playing cards."

Rosemary shook her head. "You were sitting by yourself." She looked alarmed. "We really need to get you home."

Ben shook his head. He'd had a long chat with Sheila the day before. She'd told him it was up to him, but she'd help him do it if he wanted to. It had taken a sleepless night, but he'd finally come to a decision. He hadn't known what it was, but Moses had kind of shown him the way. And yeah, it had to do with the cutting. And not wanting to get back into that habit, if he could avoid it. At least for now.

"I'm not going home. Not with you."

2019

Mangere Bridge

So I'm crouched up by the entrance in my army blanket. Supposedly I'm keeping an eye out for Thin-Lips, but mostly I'm just watching the rain.

And I'm thinking about how it must have felt to be Hape, on the turtle. It sounds good, magical ride and all, but I bet it wasn't. Cold and wet and afraid of slipping off.

I've decided since I saw Thin- Lips, I'm going to stop pretending any more. I might not be trans. But who knows except me? And I'm not afraid of anyone calling me a girl. He thought he was insulting me, but actually it felt great. Made me stop wanting to argue about it inside all the time, put on my lippy and let the world see who I really am. So thanks, Thin Lips, think you've actually done me a favour.

I'm just sitting on the drystone wall by the edge of the camp-site, thinking it through, when all of a sudden there's this cheer from behind me. I tear my eyes away from the thrilling sight of the old plastics factory, and turn round.

They've done it. They've bloody done it. A group got behind the lines of police. Snuck around the back, found a way in. And they carried a giant Tino flag, the same one we put down in front of the police line at the dawn raid. The one that stopped them moving forward, kept them where they were umtil we'd sorted reinforcements, formed our own frontline. So now they've only gone and put it like a magical carpet of daisies or the like, across the top of the hill. It's huge. Boss sized. You could probably see it from space.

So the cops are looking baffled like they don't know what to do. And I know it won't last, the hill won't be ours for long. Tomorrow they'll think up some dirty trick and drive us off again. But just for now, we're on top.

It feels good, like realising you're a girl.

1863

Port Waikato

Matua was hunched over an almost-new net, pretending it needed repair. He glanced up as Thomas approached, then looked down again.

"What do you want?" His voice was harsh.

"I thought maybe we might go fishing sometime."

Matua shook his head. "Too busy these days for that."

Thomas sat down next to him, as if he'd been invited. The river beach gravel tickled his bum. Stones. Fossils. Where it had all began.

"You coming back to school?"

Matua didn't bother to respond.

"Well, fine." Thomas shrugged. "I just wanted to say, you – when we were in the hotel, and you said –"

Matua's skin flushed darkly. "What about it?"

"You said I wasn't ready to decide who I lay with, and you weren't going to let Mr James decide for me." Thomas set his teeth together, and let the breath hiss between them like a taniwha's sigh. Matua shrugged, his scowl a mask of distrust.

"Well, I am now."

"Am now what?" Matua's voice rose in a petulant shout. "Don't you have anything better to do than hang around bothering me?"

Thomas held his gaze. "No, that's the point. I don't." He paused. "You and your dad are wrong. We don't have to wait. I'm ready to decide. And I want to. I want to lie with you."

Matua whistled softly. "I see," he said.

I needn't tell you the next part. Let's just say I remember it better than I remember what I had for breakfast today, or what the newspapers are saying about the European war.

I never did marry. Or farm. Matua, he never went off to join the war. Not everything was easy. It never is, when you choose to live that way. But we had each other, and for quite a while, that was enough.

2019

Auckland

"Hey, mum."

Cynthia looked up at Adele with a smile.

"How are you?"

"Good."

She wasn't, really, but no point in upsetting her.

"I'm good too."

Adele knew that was a lie, because her mother's eyes were sad. She sat down, and tried to pretend that she was not squatting on a chair made for a three year old. The supervised contact centre was designed like a kindergarten. The doors locked, and there were several rows of them. All this to make sure that she didn't try to run away with Mum.

"So, I've been reading a lot of Dickens to occupy my mind. He's a fascinating writer, and he writes a lot about villainy. Institutional and personal evil. I've found it very helpful." Adele was a bit bewildered why when they only had one hour together a fortnight, her mother was wasting her time trying to teach her about literature. Then she realised it was a code.

"I like Dickens too. You'll remember how much I enjoyed reading him." Cynthia knew she had never read a word. Their eyes met.

"Dickens' stories are full of terrifying things that young people go through. Often in a brutal and uncaring adult world. But things always work out in the end. That is very important to remember, when you read him." Cynthia dropped her voice.

"There'll be a hearing – soon. My lawyer says we have a case. Not a strong one. But a case."

Adele knew why she whispered. You were not supposed to discuss anything controversial.

"Stop that! No whispering!" The supervisor shouted. Cynthia's eyes met hers again, ruefully. It was awful, but it was also kind of amusing. Like being told off in class with your friend.

"School's great, I really like it." Adele improvised. It was utterly untrue, school was dismally dull and repetitive, but it was the sort of thing that the contact centre supervisors would like to hear her say. They could write it in their report and then Cynthia would not get marked down for distressing her by harping on about the past.

Cynthia laughed. "Well, that's something. Maybe I should go back to work."

They looked at each other hopelessly. Impossible to have real conversations, when you were constantly being watched. The supervisor came over and whispered in Cynthia's ear. Adele could hear. "You may not whisper and you may not discuss adult issues. You must not break the rules again, or we will have to ask you to leave."

The supervisor was a grandmotherly figure. She looked as if she would rather be making tea and toast for everyone around a warm fire, than running this place.

"Say more about Dickens," Adele suggested.

Cynthia considered. "Well, of course he had a terrible time as a young boy, was imprisoned in a debtors' prison with his father. I think that made him see the world very differently from someone who had not suffered so greatly." She hesitated, looked at the supervisor and wenr on.

"I do believe that people who go through dramatic or

difficult things will either be very broken and damaged. Or very great. No way to tell which, of course."

The supervisor frowned.

"Would you like to play a game together? We have chess, or Heroes and Hammers."

Politely, Cynthia started setting up the board game.

We all want heroes to win, Adele mused. We want to them to fight injustice, kill the monster, break free. But it doesn't always work out that way. Cynthia looked like she was broken. Perhaps she was.

"I'm still meeting those friends," she said after a pause. "The support group. And we're campaigning, about that – issue I'm interested in. Got a meeting in Parliament next week."

"I love you, Mum." At least that was true.

Cynthia smiled. "Right back at ya. Love ya to the moon and back." Adele pretended not to see the tears in her eyes.

Sometimes, the only freedom left is the freedom to pretend.

2019

Ihumatao

It was a rainy day. As Sheila stopped the car, the radio announced that a group of students had been arrested for chaining themselves together in a line on the highway. They claimed to be protecting Ihumatao and also taking a stand against global capitalism.

The police commissioner was being interviewed.

This is reckless behaviour and endangers others. It is perfectly possible to protest peacefully without putting lives at risk.

Ben got out of the car, and walked up the road. Then a small red-haired figure darted up behind him.

"Hey, Ben. I'm coming too."

They walked slowly together up the road. Mark was a lot calmer now that he'd started on the Ritalin.

"You know, Mum's drinking a lot at the moment." Mark was in a chatty mood. "Every night. Dad asked her why and she said it was to drown her sins. But I think it's cause she's missing Adele. Every time she talks to Cynthia, she comes off the phone in tears."

Ben grunted.

A woman passed them, her muddy jeans squeaking as she moved. The edges of her bundle of harakeke dragged on the ground.

"Student study tent, if you've brought your work." A pair of rain-splashed glasses peered out with a cautious welcome as they passed.

They were suddenly overtaken by thin-lipped man

in a pinstriped suit, carrying an umbrella and an eager expression. He headed towards where a group of children were playing in the mud. Ben half-thought he recognised him, but hoped he was wrong.

Now they were at the barrier. A plethora of hand-painted signs, as garish as the takeaway section at a Westfield shopping mall.

"Haere mai."

"We want Jacinda."

"No police, no protest. Only protectors."

"Stay strong, knowing we are our ancestors wildest dreams."

Adele would hate that missing apostrophe, Ben thought. He noticed he was thinking about her as if she was dead. Well, perhaps she was. Since the judge and social workers had decided that, contrary to police evidence, she probably wasn't telling the truth and might as well be returned to her father after all. She'd sent a text message from school saying she'd run away again soon.

The signs leaned on packing cases, which had been piled up to create a makeshift wall. Behind them, a group of sodden volunteers crouched around an oil drum, trying to keep a reluctant fire alight. They sheltered under a gazebo lurched sideways, as if drunk on drizzle. As Mark and Ben approached, a figure wrapped in an army blanket got up to greet them.

"Kia ora, welcome." He stuck out a friendly hand. At least, Ben thought from his voice he was a he, it was hard to see in this rain.

Ben stopped, and fumbled in his backpack. He might as well do it here as anywhere else.

"Here." He stepped forward, and held out the amber-studded taiaha.

The indeterminately gendered figure in an army blanket took a step forward, then back. They looked at the taiaha with fear, as if it might bite. But they also looked with a strange longing, as if it was a taonga they'd wanted to see for the whole of their life.

"Holy crap," a young woman almost completely covered by a plastic poncho called from her safe perch inside the gazebo. "That's beautiful. What is it?"

"It's a gift. Like to say sorry. Cause his ancestors stole it." Mark helpfully clarified the situation.

There wasn't much else to say. Ben put the taiaha on the ground, and took a step back. As if afraid it would vanish, the kid in the army-blanket darted forward and picked it up. They held it in their arms and crooned, cradling it like a long-lost child.

"We've got you back, you're home..."

Awkward. "Yeah, well. See you." Ben turned around to go.

"No, wait." The young woman pushed back her crackling poncho. Riverlets of water dropped on the ground. "Come have a cup of tea."

Ben shook his head. "I've got to go. I don't – belong."

"We all belong." A jolly middle-aged wahine with a missing front tooth strolled up. "I'm just back from Australia. Haven't been home for, ooh, eleven years. Ihumatao called me. Looks like it called you too."

Ben shook his head a second time. "You're Māori . I'm an invader. Best thing I can do, get out of your way."

"Bullshit."

Ben thought wildly of Moses, blurring into nothingness and light as he walked up the corridor.

Behind them, the Manukau harbour. The place where Māori first landed in New Zealand. The beginning of the human story here, of farming and adventure and love and hunting and story telling and karakia prayer and war.

And quietly, like a lost century, beyond it, the distant sea.

A mystery, like Moses, and the box of secrets, and the truth. The universe as it is, and not as we think or wish or dream. He thought of Adele, and wished she could see it too. Perhaps one day. Life was shit, but at least they were all growing up. Things had to improve longterm. Didn't they?

Or would it all be global warming, life collapsing, no one with the time to care?

The woman who had called bullshit suddenly noticed the amber taiaha in the army blanketed arms.

"My God." She went a shuddering shade of pale. "Am I dreaming this? Is that yours?"

They glared at her defensively, as if she would try to snatch it from their arms. "It's a family taonga. Sold generations ago. My kuia told me. We've been cursed ever since."

She took a closer look. But not at the taiaha. At the youth's face.

"Fuck me. Are you, what's your name?"

The army blanket shrugged. "Hape. What's it to you?"

"Hape?" She clapped a loud hand on her mouth. "Sweet Jesus and all the saints. I think I'm your mum."

They looked at each other. Disbelief, distrust, wounded feelings and longing.

Then Hape shrugged. Their lips curled with a bitter smile.

"You expect me to believe that?"

"It's the lost taiaha. You know the story." She repeated it, word for word.

Hape shrugged. "So you know some old gossip. So? And even if you are mum, why should I care? Ten years ago might have been helpful. But now, it's a bit late."

"No, wait. I know what you think. But I didn't, I didn't know. About the court." The words flooded out of her like rain. "I never got the letter. When I did, they said it was too late. Case already heard. Couldn't bear it without you. Went over to Australia. Had more kids there."

The rain dripped down her nose. Hape hesitated, raised their fist to punch the air, let it fall again.

"You for real?"

"Course I am. As real as you. Soon as I saw the taiaha I knew."

There was an awkward pause, as if neither of them knew what to do. Then, arms flapping, Hape lunged forward and hugged her.

"Well." The poncho wearer clapped her hands. "I'd say this calls for a celebration. See, now you two will have to stay."

A messy-haired woman ambled past, her unicorn blanket sodden in the rain. "Does anyone want me to tell them a story?"

"Oh, do piss off back to Disneyworld," Hape's mother snapped. "And what the shit should we celebrate with out here? Rain? Cold tea?"

Hape sniffed, and wiped their nose. "Yeah. We can celebrate when we've won."

They looked at their mother. "Guess now we've gotta try not to mess each other up. Any more than both of us already are."

Another silence. Broken by Mark.

"We gotta go. Mum's waiting in the car."

They walked back silently. A short distance from the barrier, the thin-lipped man stood still and angry, between two cops. He had lost his umbrella, and his expensive pinstriped suit was sagging shapelessly in the rain. Above, his angular features trembled with rage. One police officer held his arm, whilst the other read aloud ponderously from a text on his phone.

"Mr Bernard James. You are under arrest. You have the right to remain silent. A warrant, issued by Howick Constabulary in 1862 – sorry, that must be a misprint, let's say 2016 – on suspicion of having committed gross indecency against a number of young people, male and female - "

Ben and Mark stopped to listen, but the police officer shooed them on.

Reluctantly, they headed back toward the public road. Where the fairytale ends, and the waking world begins again.

A couple of ageing police officers met them on the way, and greeted the boys politely. Because it was raining, and none of them really wanted to be there, and actually, those idiots at the council had made the wrong decision in the first place, and the more you hung out here, you saw that the protest movement wasn't just a mindless rabble, it was a bunch of kids and grannies with soul.

Mark and Ben walked on. As their feet hit the tarmac, both turned. One last look at the whenua. Like the final moments of a book, when even the most captivated reader knows it's time to leave the fiction be, say goodbye to the dream.

And there, of course, they were, just as they had both hoped. Hape, hugging her mum. Papatuanuku, fluttering the great flag on the hill. And behind them both, Kupe, paddling past on the deep. A fish jumped, somewhere between today and tomorrow. Then it disappeared, into the silent remembering sea.